Praise for Sticky Wicket Vol. 1

"Sticky Wicket, Vol. 1, Watkins At Bat is a wonderful addition to contemporary cricket literature. The plot weaves the age-old themes of the sport into modern life... This first volume is a strong opener for what should be a successful series."
-Paul Hensley, *president of C.C. Morris Cricket Library at Haverford College in Haverford, Pennsylvania, the largest depository of cricket memorabilia in the Western Hemisphere.*

*

"To the cricket-initiated, the volume is distilled mirth."
- Tom Baldwin, Gannett News Service, and author of *"Big Storm, Small Ship."*

*

"The scheming plots involved in getting some of the players, both young and old, away from their wives to the playing field...will surely give any reader who enjoys a good laugh lots to laugh about."
- Carol Quash, *Trinidad Guardian*

*

"A bit of Watkins resides in all our hearts and homes. An entertaining narrative about the interaction of cricketing families in the United States, chronicled in a jocular way that makes reading *Sticky Wicket* fun and a must read for all cricket enthusiasts."
- Shelton Glasgow, *president, Garden State Cricket League; regional director, Atlantic Region of the United States of America Cricket Association, and USACA board member.*

*

"*Watkins At Bat* is an entertaining romp with a motley cast of characters by an author whose love of the game of cricket is evident on every page. A wonderful adventure!"
- Glenn Walker, owner/moderator of Writer Circle:
http://groups.yahoo.com/group/writercircle/

*

"The author has used his favorite game as a metaphor to bring his feisty characters to life in a sparkling and humorous manner

that is a delight. Ride along with Rouse's imagination in *Sticky Wicket, Vol. 1, Watkins At Bat,* and hurry; the 'cricket train' is about to leave the station. Be on it!"
- Paul Gordon, *author of "Concrete Solution" "Van Gogh's Last Painting" and "Bogey-man on Gaston Street."*

*

"It was hilarious reading how these fellows got away from their wives on Sundays to enjoy a game that we all grew up playing. I also was moved to see how cricket brought so many different races together."
- Adrian Rahim, *captain, Jersey City Cricket Club, Jersey City, New Jersey.*

*

"I read the novel during a flight from Philadelphia to Jamaica and laughed so hard, and so often, that passengers near me must have thought I had lost it."
- Paul Francis, *co-founder, Echelon Cricket Club, Voorhees, New Jersey.*

*

"I thought I was reliving my playing experiences in America while reading of the exploits of Frederick Watkins. It was hard to put down once I started it. I finished the book in one sitting. I was glad I didn't have to go out to bat during that time!"
- Dan Ruparel, *president, The Littleton Cricket Club and Colorado Junior Cricket Association, and former president Colorado Cricket League.*

*

"Though the novel may, at first, seem simply to entail a game of cricket, it embraces much more. The theme of power permeates it: power in the home, power on the field, power for the field."
--Myrtle Aberdeen, *literary critic.*

*

"I enjoyed reading this first volume quite a bit and look forward to reading further volumes."
Ron Knight, *umpire, Mid-Atlantic Cricket Conference, Chapel Hill, North Carolina.*

EWART ROUSE

STICKY WICKET

VOL. 2

watkins fights back

All LMH titles, imprints and distributed lines are available at special quantity discounts for bulk purchases for sales promotion, premiums, fund-raising, educational or institutional use.

Cover design: Sanya Dockery
Cover illustration: Clovis Brown
Book design, layout & typesetting: Sanya Dockery

Published by LMH Publishing Limited
Suite 10-11
LOJ Industrial Complex
7 Norman Road
Kingston C.S.O., Jamaica
Tel.: (876) 938-0005; 938-0712
Fax: (876) 759-8752
Email: lmhbookpublishing@cwjamaica.com
Website: www.lmhpublishing.com

Printed in the U. S. A.   ISBN:978-976-8202-55-0

This book is dedicated to all cricket lovers out there fighting for a place to play the game of their youth in the land of baseball.

Acknowledgments

The author wishes to thank the following people for their invaluable contributions: Ben Acosta, Porus Cooper, Margo Foster, Fran Metzman, Maryliz Clark, Danny Patel and Amber Samaroo.

FOREWORD

When immigrants from the West Indies, India, Pakistan and England settle in Fernwood, South Jersey, USA, they want to play the game of their youth: cricket. The obstacles they face are the theme of the Sticky Wicket trilogy, *Watkins At Bat*, *Watkins Fights Back* and *Watkins' Final Inning*.

Not only must Frederick A. Watkins, the protagonist who is of West Indian heritage, fight with his African-American wife, Gina, to spend his weekends on the cricket field, he and his ragtag team from many lands must vie with local officials of the suburban town who prefer that only Little League baseball teams play on their field.

In addition to facing the challenges of prejudice and political opportunists, the Fernwood Cricket Club must also wrestle with the problem of aging players, personal foibles and distractions, and pull of family who want their time and affection.

How Watkins juggles a cast of multi-ethnic, multi-national characters from all walks of life to keep the cricket club alive, and his marriage intact, leads the reader through a true "sticky wicket."

watkins fights back

CHAPTER 1

Monday, April 30

It was the morning after his team's season opener and, instead of getting up early and crowing about his heroics in that cricket game, Freddie Watkins was lying late in bed with a splitting headache.

The scorebook showed that he was his team's last man at bat, with the opposition score seemingly beyond reach, but that he had pulled off a spectacular win for his team with a flurry of big hits with his beloved bat.

The victory was no mean feat. Fernwood Cricket Club, after all, had the worst record in the history of the New Jersey Cricket League, while its opponent, Jamaica Rebels Cricket Club, was the perennial champion.

It was a classic case of a lowly David knocking off the mighty Goliath.

But the scorebook didn't tell the full story. It didn't show that teammate Harold Richardson Minster, the old man of the side at 64, suffered a massive heart attack after helping Watkins score those winning runs and that "Pops" now lay in a coma in a hospital.

It didn't reflect the confrontation Watkins and his teammates had with one Maximilian Kruger, the president of the Fernwood Little League, over rights to the grounds.

Nor did the scorebook record the fistfight that broke out at the end of the game between the captain of the Jamaica Rebels and Napoleon Bonaparte, an ex-professional Jamaican player whom Fernwood hired for the game because it was short of players.

And, perhaps most damaging of all, the scorebook didn't show the showdown between Watkins and his wife, with Gina accusing him of breaking the solemn promise he had made to her last season that he would retire from the sport and begin accompanying her to church on Sundays.

And now, here he was, late Monday morning after the game from hell, still in bed with a ferocious headache, his sore muscles telling him his wife was right when she had lectured him that, with his 55th birthday days away, he wasn't a teenager anymore, and it was time he started acting his age.

A ringing sound broke through Watkins' reverie.

Sifting through the haze in his brain, Watkins deduced that it was the doorbell.

Gina was in the shower.

With an effort, Watkins used both hands to lift stiff legs over the edge of the bed, lowered them gently onto the floor, and gradually straightened up, his body creaking like a door with rusty hinges. He shuffled up to a front window and pushed it open.

The postman was at the front door. "Need you to sign for a certified letter," he announced.

"I'll be right down," Watkins said, closed the window and began swinging his body back and forth like an aerobics dancer, trying to get the creaks out, before making his way down the hallway and a flight of steps to the front door.

The letter was from the Office of the Mayor, Fernwood Township, and addressed to Frederick A. Watkins, manager, Fernwood Cricket Club.

Watkins signed for the missive, slipped the clipboard back to the postman, and quietly shut the front door. He started to retreat on tiptoes down the steps to his basement office, looked up and froze.

Gina, wrapped in a red robe, her hair all wet, stood rigidly at the top of the steps. He sensed that his wife was there the moment he opened the door, monitoring his every movement.

Suspicious eyes dropped to the letter and her brows furrowed. "That wouldn't be from your cricket buddies, would it?"

"No, Gina," Watkins replied, with a deliberate sigh intended to convey that her accusatory tone was unwarranted, even as he shielded the letter by pressing it against his body. "After causing you so much grief yesterday, I'm now permanently retired. I plan to communicate that decision to my so-called cricket buddies in clear, unambiguous language."

"Don't forget to tell them of your decision to join the men's choir and to be baptized."

"One thing at a time, Gina," he said, with an even heavier sigh, and proceeded to his basement office.

Secure in his private space, Watkins listened to his wife's receding footsteps overhead. Only when all was quiet did he feel safe to open the envelope. The letter stated:

Dear Mr. Watkins,

When the township granted the Fernwood Cricket Club permission to use the George Washington Middle School grounds for its home games, you were provided with a copy of the rules and regulations pertaining to park usage.

It has been brought to my attention that one of your players, a Napoleon Bonaparte, violated those rules and regulations during your game yesterday by threatening the public safety. In light of the flagrant violation, your club's permission to use the school grounds is hereby rescinded, effective immediately.

Sincerely,

Neil Quigley, mayor

After the confrontation with the Little League president over who had rights to the middle school grounds and the man's threats to take his complaint to Quigley, Watkins expected the fallout, but not *this* soon. Quigley must have penned his letter overnight, was the first one in the door when the post office opened, and used his clout to make sure it was delivered promptly.

Although expecting the fallout, Watkins felt slighted. At the very least, the mayor could have offered some semblance of fairness by seeking his side of the story before kicking the cricket club off the middle school grounds.

Under normal circumstances, Watkins would have relished taking on City Hall, but he had put away his cricket gear for good. Others would have to take up the challenge.

Ewart Rouse

Watkins flipped open his cell phone and dialed the law firm of Emile Pierre.

"Bad news," Watkins announced when the club president and team captain picked up, and proceeded to read the letter.

"They've got to the kidding," Pierre said when Watkins was through. "We've been playing cricket in Fernwood for twenty-five years. Where does the mayor get off telling us we can't continue?"

"So, what are *you* going to do about it?"

"We were assigned the middle school grounds by the township recreation director; it would be a breach of contract to kick us off," Pierre said.

"The assignment wasn't in writing."

"Doesn't matter," Pierre said. "An oral contract is just as good. We'll just have to sue for breach of contract."

Spoken like a lawyer, Watkins thought. "We sue and it will be months, maybe years, before the case is heard."

"We first seek a temporary restraining order, barring anyone from using the grounds pending a hearing on the merits of our lawsuit. That would shake them up."

"Before we resort to any legal action, we should at least try to resolve this peacefully," Watkins advised. "Sit down with the mayor. I'm sure he'll be able to work something out."

"I'm a one-man law firm and I don't have time for this PR bull," Pierre said. "They screw with us, we take them to court. That's the American way. If you want to play Mr. Nice Guy to The Man, then *you* go meet with him."

"You know I can't."

"Gina doesn't have to know about it," Pierre said.

"Maneuver behind her back?" Watkins laughed at the thought. "That would be deceiving her. I don't want to do that."

"Then be upfront with her. Tell her you have to do this one last assignment for the club."

Watkins laughed louder. "That was my excuse for coming out of retirement for yesterday's game, and it almost wrecked my marriage."

"Tell her you couldn't have anticipated our losing the grounds," said Pierre, in that lawyer-to-client advisory tone. "She cares about you, doesn't she?"

"Very much so," he said with self-assurance.

"If she truly loves you, then she wouldn't want you to be miserable watching the cricket club go down the tubes and not being allowed to lift a finger to stop it. She won't want that on *her* conscience."

"You don't know Gina," Watkins said, no longer thinking it a laughing matter. "She wasn't born in the Islands as we were, so she doesn't understand why the game is so important to us. She was born in this country and grew up in the church. For twenty-five years she has put up with me deserting her on Sundays, carrying on as if I were a nineteen-year-old with no responsibilities."

Now Pierre was the one chuckling. "Is that what she tells you?"

"That's just the tip of the iceberg."

"How come you married an African American woman anyway? West Indian women weren't good enough for you?"

"Don't go there," Watkins said, disappointed at Pierre for going there. "Never go there."

"Sorry. I know you love your wife..."

"I do love my wife," Watkins said, emphasizing the word *love*. "Very much so. If I don't quit this game Gina will divorce me for sure, and I'll end up at Ancora."

He said it as a joke, but he actually could see it happening. Gina had been such a part of his life since the day he met the pastor's daughter that her leaving conceivably could push him into the state mental hospital.

"If you want, I'll give Gina a call."

"Leave Gina out of this," Watkins said, now a little annoyed at Pierre's persistence. "You're the club president and team captain, and you're an attorney. That makes you the club leader. So lead for a change."

"I've been leader in name only," Pierre acknowledged. "You've been the club manager for the longest while, the one who actually ran the organization."

"Used to run the organization," Watkins corrected. "Past tense."

"Look, I'm due in court and I'm late. Talk to The Man. Let me know how it turns out. If he insists on denying us a place to play, it would take me only a half-hour to file that restraining order."

Watkins hung up, disappointed, but not really surprised. Like the rest of the bunch, all Pierre wanted to know was where the next game was. He was a leader on the field only.

Mulling over the club's predicament, Watkins rationalized that there was no real harm in giving the mayor a call. That didn't constitute any breach of *his* promise to Gina to stay retired, did it?

He dialed the mayor's number, got the township clerk, and asked for Quigley.

"Mr. Quigley's in a meeting and cannot be disturbed," she said.

Watkins then dialed the township recreation director.

"Guess you got the bad news," Joseph Sarubbi said.

"That the Fernwood Cricket Club, the granddaddy of sporting organizations in Fernwood, is no longer welcomed in its birthplace?" Watkins said with sarcasm. "How come you didn't give me a heads-up?"

"Now learning about it, Partner," Sarubbi said, in his typical cavalier manner.

Watkins heard footsteps overhead.

"I'll have to call you back," he said, slipped the letter into the envelope, tucked the envelope into his desk drawer, and resumed editing of his novel-in-progress on the computer screen.

Gina entered his space, her hair in place, dressed in a light spring coat.

"Thought you were still in pain," she said, eyes wandering across his desktop.

"I am, but not bedridden."

Wandering eyes refocused on him. "So, what was that certified mail all about?"

The beep-beep of a car horn sounded outside.

"That's probably Mary," Gina said.

And none too soon, Watkins thought. "Where are you guys off to today?"

"Have you forgotten? Today is the Amway products meeting at the Chamber of Commerce building."

"You guys are really serious about going into business for yourselves, aren't you?"

"We'll just hear what the products manager has to say before we decide," she said.

"Well, have fun."

"There's a bottle of extra-strength Excedrin in the medicine cabinet if you need it."

"I should be fine," he said, rising to usher her out and up the steps to the front door.

The women waved as they drove off. Watkins waved back, waited until the Hyundai had left the cul-de-sac, then returned to his basement space.

"We need to talk," he told Sarubbi on the call back.

"I'm about to leave the office now on an errand. Why don't you meet me down at the school grounds in, say, twenty minutes?"

"I'll be there," Watkins said, figuring that it would be another couple of hours before Gina arrived home from her sales meeting. He should be back by then.

******

After getting dressed and into his wagon in slow motion, Watkins drove to the George Washington Middle School grounds across town. Classes were in progress. On the grounds, across from the school, men were peering through surveying equipment and taking measurements.

Standing outside his wagon, Watkins heard the blast of a motorcycle and watched Sarubbi ride up on a Harley-Davidson. Sarubbi was a slightly built, middle-aged man with long sideburns. His penchant for cycles and long weekend rides with his live-in girlfriend was a recent phenomenon that everyone said was part of the daredevil phase men go through in seeking to roll the clock back.

"Howdy, Partner," Sarubbi said, pulling up alongside the Volkswagen wagon and raising his hand for a high-five.

Watkins slapped his hand. "What's going on here?" he said, jerking his head in the direction of the men on the grounds with the surveying equipment.

"It is what it looks like; they're preparing to put up a fence," Sarubbi said.

"To keep us out?"

"To keep you out, and Little League in," Sarubbi said, propping himself against the bike and folding his arms. "I got a copy of the letter that was sent to you by the mayor. Tell me about your clash with Max Kruger, the police, Napoleon Bonaparte, the whole nine yards."

Watkins steadied himself for the painful recitation: "We were nearing the end of our game when Maximilian Kruger showed up. He said he needed the grounds for a Little League game. We told him you had given us permission to use the grounds. He said the grounds belonged to Little League and we had better get off before he called the cops. When we refused to leave he made some derogatory remarks about us, then the cops showed up. We explained that our game was almost finished and, after a little back-and-forth, they allowed us to complete it. Kruger berated the cops for not kicking us off, then told us we'd be hearing from the mayor."

"Sounds like Max was really throwing his weight around," said Sarubbi. "Now tell me about this Napoleon Bonaparte character. Who is he and what did he do to *threaten the public safety?*"

"Napoleon is a former professional cricket player from Jamaica," Watkins began, and there was an acrid taste in his mouth as he uttered the name. "He's like a mercenary, going around selling his services to cricket clubs on the day of their games. We had trouble putting a team together for our game. He showed up and we paid him to play for us."

"How much?"

"Two hundred bucks," Watkins said, mad at himself anew for making the payment against his better judgment.

"You paid this hired gun two hundred dollars and he ends up muddying the waters for your club. Tell me how he did that."

"The game was over and the players were leaving when Napoleon and the captain of the Jamaica Rebels got into an argument," Watkins said, uneasy at recounting the incident but figuring that he might as well because there probably was a police record of it. "The two men apparently have a rivalry that goes back to their playing days in Ocho Rios and Kingston. The Jamaica Rebels captain knocked Napoleon down with a punch to the jaw. Napoleon threatened to go home, get his gun and come back and shoot everybody."

"That's serious," Sarubbi said.

"He was only grandstanding, trying to save face after being knocked down."

"Were the cops still there?"

"They were," Watkins recalled. "They must have witnessed the incident and stopped and questioned Napoleon as he was leaving."

"It seems to me that our mayor is using the Napoleon incident as a smoke screen to allow Max Kruger to have his way," Sarubbi said.

"That's pretty obvious," Watkins said, reassured at having Sarubbi in his corner.

Sarubbi withdrew his copy of the letter, read it as if looking for a loophole, and returned it to his pocket. "Our mayor is citing a provision in our park rules and regulations that makes the clubs accountable for any misconduct by their members on the field. But, according to what you're telling me, this Napoleon character wasn't a member of your club. He was a gun for hire..."

"A visiting player," Watkins corrected him.

"A visiting player," Sarubbi adopted his terminology. "Once the game was over, so was the contract between your club and Napoleon. The incident you described didn't occur during the game and Napoleon no longer was associated with your club. No way could your club be held liable for his actions."

If there was one person in township government Watkins knew he could count on to give the cricket club a fair shake, it would be Sarubbi. Watkins had known the recreation director since the formation of the cricket club and they had worked well together. The big question was whether Sarubbi had the clout to get the mayor to reverse his decision.

Sarubbi climbed back onto the bike. "Quigley normally meets with members of the planning and zoning boards on Monday morning. Let me run my errand, then try to see whether I can corner him before he takes off. Can you come to my office in an hour?"

"I can be there."

"I'll see you then," Sarubbi replied, and looked past him. "Speaking of Mr. Heavyweight..."

Watkins turned and saw a sporty looking red Pontiac GTO racing toward them. It squealed to a stop at the curb about a hundred feet away from one of the men surveying the school grounds. Maximilian Kruger alighted.

A wave of anger washed over Watkins as he watched the Little League chief, who was dressed the way he was yesterday, in a green warm-up sweatsuit with the words *Fernwood Little League* on the chest and the association's logo of a fern stitched across the left shoulder.

"Don't worry," Sarubbi said, revving up his bike. "I'll take care of you guys. Ciao, Partner."

As Sarubbi blasted off. Watkins studied Kruger as he peered through a piece of the surveying equipment. He mentally revisited his confrontation with the Little League chief and wondered whether he had handled it badly. The man had pushed and he had reacted instinctively by pushing back, and now Kruger was showing just how much weight he carried in the affluent suburban township.

Perhaps he should have a little chitchat with Kruger, one athlete to another.

Watkins approached cautiously and waited for Kruger to turn his way.

"Can we talk it over?" he said, when Kruger finally did.

"I did warn you people," Kruger said, muttered something in German, and showed him his back.

Watkins saw the futility of further exchange. For Kruger, the battle already had been fought and won; the decision to put up fences to keep the cricket club out was irreversible.

Watkins got back in his wagon and headed for the Fernwood Township Library.

******

After scouting out the library shelves, Watkins checked out two books relating to his nascent novel-writing career, John Gardner's *The Art of Fiction* and Percy Lubbock's *The Craft of Fiction*.

With another half-hour to kill, Watkins drove a few streets away to the Southern New Jersey Hospital, Fernwood Division.

After convincing the receptionist in the lobby that he was like family to "Pops," the receptionist called the supervisor on the intensive-care floor. She reported back that Harold Richardson Minster was still in a coma.

Wracked with guilt over his decision to take "Pops" to the game because they were short, Watkins headed for his 12:15 meeting with Sarubbi.

He found Sarubbi in his corner office in the Office of Community Recreation, with its wall-to-wall trophies and commendations from a host of clubs, including Fernwood Cricket Club.

"Max Kruger wasn't bluffing," Sarubbi announced the moment Watkins walked in. "After his run-in with the cricket club, he went straight to the mayor, making noise about you guys."

"What sort of noise?"

"Who you are, where you come from."

Watkins was struck by the irony of the whole thing. "Max Kruger and the Little Leaguers move into Fernwood and want to know who are these black and brown people with foreign accents in white clothes playing this strange game on *their* grounds?"

"That's about the size of it."

"Unbelievable," Watkins sighed.

"Believe it," Sarubbi said. "I told Quigley you guys started playing cricket here back when Fernwood was mostly apple and peach farms. Hell, I once played with you guys."

"You did," Watkins said, and had a flashback of the direct hit to the crotch with a fastball that ended Sarubbi's short-lived experiment with the cricket bat. "What did Quigley say when you told him we shouldn't be held accountable for Napoleon's behavior?"

"He changed his tune," Sarubbi said.

"What's he saying now?"

"You'll be getting a new letter in the mail," Sarubbi confided. "This one will say that with the rapid growth of Little League baseball and kids' soccer, grounds are at a premium right now. The township and school board policy is that the kids get priority in the use of the grounds. On that basis, the George Washington Middle School grounds are being assigned exclusively to Little League."

Watkins had his doubts that Sarubbi could get the mayor to reverse himself, but there had been a sliver of hope. The crushing of that hope was like the punch that the Jamaica Rebels captain had delivered to Napoleon's jaw: staggering.

He doubled over onto a side chair. "What about adult soccer, baseball, softball, field hockey, rugby, lacrosse? Are their grounds also being reassigned to Little League and kids' soccer?"

"Not that I know of."

"Then why is cricket being singled out?"

"You figure."

"Because we're different?" Watkins didn't think he needed to say more.

"The fact that most of the cricket members are people of color may be part of it, but certainly not the biggest part."

"Kruger called us outsiders," Watkins remembered. "Told us this wasn't Africa or India."

"That's ironic, considering that he's also an immigrant, with an accent so thick you'd swear he just got off the boat," Sarubbi said. "Look, where you come from is only part of your problem. Believe me, if you were the Daughters of the American Revolution, the Sons of Italy, the VFW, or the Garden Club of New Jersey, Maximilian Kruger would run you over just as fast if he thought he could get away with it. The tragedy is that Quigley is letting him get away with it."

"If not race, or nationality, what?" Watkins said.

"The real problem is votes. You don't have the votes."

"What do you mean?"

"Come here." Sarubbi led him to a back window, and drew the slats aside. "Look out there on those lawns. What do you see?"

Sarubbi was referring to two competing political signs on the lawns of the residential development across the street.

One said: NO TIME FOR CHANGE - *Vote Tuesday June 12 — Neil Quigley for Mayor.*

The other said: TIME FOR CHANGE - *Vote Tuesday, June 12 - Councilwoman Andrea Grimes for Mayor.*

"What about it?" Watkins asked.

"Maybe you haven't noticed, but there's an election going on," Sarubbi said, drawing the slats back in place. "Quigley's running for a full term on the slogan that this is *No Time For Change*. His challenger, Grimes, is saying *It's Time For Change*. And Max Kruger holds the fate of both candidates in the palm of his hands."

"How's that?"

"Max Kruger's pitch," Sarubbi said, "is that Fernwood Little League has two thousand members. Each member has two parents. That's four thousand votes. With that kind of power, Max Kruger gets whatever Max Kruger wants. By the way, you aren't hearing any of this from me."

Watkins pledged with a nod to keep it between them.

"My view," Sarubbi continued, a bit heatedly, "and I've told Quigley as much, is that if you get rid of cricket this year, it would be girls' softball next year, and kids' soccer the year after, and pretty soon the Little League would have run over all the grounds like beavers through a wood pile. Little League has grown to the point where it's time for it to start thinking of purchasing its own grounds."

Watkins never had cause to accuse the township of bias against his club or its members. On the contrary, Sarubbi had thrown out the welcome mat to the club and had proven a friend throughout its long history, ensuring that the cricket wicket was well-maintained and the grass was cut on game days. Now, for the first time, Watkins felt the sting of the outsider label.

"We've lived here for many, many years," he lamented. "All we have ever asked as good citizens is for a little patch of green to play the game of our youth. In this big and wealthy township, I don't think that's asking too much."

"I hear you, Partner," Sarubbi said.

"But, tell me, isn't the Board of Education the one in charge of school grounds?" He asked the question, though he knew this to be a fact. "If the board doesn't want us using the George Washington Middle School grounds to play cricket, shouldn't the school superintendent be the one writing to us?"

"You've got that right," Sarubbi said. "The school board is supposed to be in charge of school grounds and the township government in charge of township-owned grounds. The reality is that Quigley and the president of the school board, and everybody who is anybody in this township, are all connected, either by blood or political affiliation, with Quigley calling the shots. He's the big dog in town. He says poop, they all squat."

"Does that include you?" Watkins said, in good humor.

Sarubbi took it the right way, with a laugh. "I do the scheduling for both school property and township-owned grounds because it's convenient to have one person do so. But I'm a political appointee, answerable to the mayor. He can big-foot me any time he chooses, and he has chosen to do so in this instance."

"And you're telling me there's nothing you can do for us?"

Sarubbi went up to a side wall. On it was a large chart with a listing of the fifteen school board and township-owned grounds. It showed what teams had been assigned to them from April through September.

"There are some open Saturdays," Sarubbi noted.

"We play Sunday league," Watkins said.

Sarubbi studied the chart some more. "As you can see, Sunday afternoons are booked solid. What about Sunday mornings? I can squeeze you in from 9 to noon."

"Under league rules, our cricket games start at 1 p.m. and normally go until 7."

"That's the problem with cricket," Sarubbi said, sighing. "You need the field for most of the day because your game is two to three times as long as a regular softball or football game."

"I don't think we should be penalized because of the length of the game."

"There's one option you might want to consider," Sarubbi said. "Have you ever thought of owning your own grounds?"

Owning? "The question has never come up."

Sarubbi's secretary appeared to remind him of another meeting.

"I better get going," Sarubbi said to Watkins. "I'll be riding past a piece of ground I'd like to show you. Why don't you follow me?"

******

The ground in question was among the last undeveloped tracts of land at the southernmost part of town. It reminded Watkins of the raw ground to which the cricket club was assigned a quarter-century ago when the township was still the sticks.

"It belongs to a college roommate of mine in Miami," Sarubbi explained as they stood in the narrow dirt road fronting the property. "His father died a couple of months back and left it to him. He's about to put it on the market. If you're interested, I can have a word with him for you before the *For Sale* sign goes up."

"What's the asking price?"

"The property is assessed at twenty-five grand, but that's half its market value," Sarubbi said.

"Fifty grand? We're an amateur club. We don't have that kind of cash."

"You're talking three acres of prime real estate," Sarubbi said. "There's enough room for a ball field and clubhouse. You guys are business minded, aren't you? When not using them, you could rent out the field and the clubhouse for functions. The rental income pays your mortgage and gives you something extra in your kitty. The way real estate is appreciating these days, the facility would be worth a fortune down the line."

Watkins scanned the property with fresh eyes. Sarubbi was right about rising values of real estate. The club would have been sitting pretty if members had had the foresight to buy back when it was founded.

"I suppose it makes sense, but you're talking fifty grand to buy the land, then at least two hundred thousand dollars to build a decent clubhouse," Watkins said. "We'll have to win the lottery to afford that."

"You guys have good collateral, don't you?" Sarubbi said. "You pool the collateral in your homes and businesses to buy the land, build on it, and you're set for life."

"I can run it by the guys, but I doubt they'd be willing to take that leap," Watkins said.

"It's something to think about," Sarubbi said. "But don't take too long to make a decision. Once it's listed, developers will snap up this property in a heartbeat."

"In the meantime, what do we do about our home games?"

"Why don't you take your case to the Township Council?" Sarubbi suggested. "The council meets the first

Tuesday in the month. The next meeting is tomorrow night."

"What good would that do when Quigley controls the council?"

"Go make some noise anyway," Sarubbi said. "Squeaky wheels get the grease." Sarubbi straddled his Harley-Davidson. "Ciao, Partner."

******

Watkins arrived home at 1:45 p.m. to find Gina in the backyard in jeans with the legs rolled up and plastic garden boots. He could tell from the way she yanked the dead stalks of her veggie garden that she was in a foul mood.

"How did your Amway meeting go?"

"Pops' wife called," she said. "She wanted me to know that you were the one who dragged her husband out to the game yesterday. Said you waited until she had left for church to go to her home to pick Pops up. She said if he dies it will be your fault."

"Pops is a grown man," Watkins heard himself say, trying to suppress his anger at Mrs. Minster. He had reached out to the woman, taking it upon himself to break the news to her of Pops' collapse at the grounds, driving her to and from the hospital. Why drag Gina into it? "I went to the Minsters' home to pick up some bats that Pops had repaired for the club. I invited him to come out to the game and he came out. No one forced him to do anything."

"He's an old man, a very, very sick, old man." Gina faced him then and he could tell from the redness in her eyes that she had been crying. "Good Lord, what is the matter with you, Fred?"

"Look, I feel bad enough...."

She picked up a spade and he jumped back. Had it come to this? She shoved the tool into the earth and tried to turn the soil. The wooden handle snapped.

The tears came in torrents. "Oh, Fred, I'm so scared for you!"

His anger subsided. Pops' heart attack had frightened Gina, had made her cognizant of his mortality. "I'm sorry."

"Where were you?"

"I went to the library to do some research for my book," he said, holding up as proof the two books he had checked out. "Afterward, I went to the hospital to check on Pops' condition. I'm sorry if I upset you. It won't happen again."

Watkins headed to the house.

"Fred," she called after him, "wherever you took my rake, my shovel and my broom, please bring them back!"

He had forgotten the tools, used to prepare yesterday's wicket, in the wagon. He got them for her and would have joined her in gardening but thought it best to allow her to cool off alone.

The phone rang as he entered the house.

He picked up in the family room.

"Big Daddy," cracked the voice at the other end. "Emergency meeting of the club. At my house. Six o'clock sharp."

Watkins peered through the blinds, making sure Gina was still in the garden before replying. "What's up?"

"You've put me in big, big trouble," Raj Bhattacharya said, dragging out the word *big*.

Watkins apologized for the head injury that Bhattacharya's son suffered while fielding for Fernwood during the game.

"This has nothing to do with your taking my son to the game," Bhattacharya said. "If the boy wants to play cricket, he has to learn to get hit."

"Then what is it?"

"Just get everybody here."

Watkins had known Maharaj Bhattacharya as a gregarious man whose generosity to the club was boundless. Something extraordinary had to have caused him to be this agitated.

"I'll see what I can do," Watkins said, unwilling to make any promises.

Watkins retreated to his basement office, closed the door, and made a call to Emile Pierre's law firm.

The club leader was back from his court hearing.

First, he briefed Pierre on his meeting with Joe Sarubbi.

"He wants us to shell out fifty grand for a piece of property?" Pierre said. "Is that the best he can come up with?"

"Like he said, it's something to put in the back of your mind."

"I say we file that injunction."

"Not yet," Watkins said, knowing his word was still law. "Suing should always be our last resort. Do as Sarubbi suggests and go to the Township Council meeting tomorrow night. See what comes out of it."

"Okay, we'll play it your way, but you definitely should be there."

"I'll see if I can swing it," Watkins said, unwilling to commit himself.

Watkins then recounted his conversation with Bhattacharya.

Pierre was just as puzzled about the "big trouble" that they had caused their financial benefactor.

So, too, were the other club members he called.

Last on his list of people to call was Vijay Patel.

He telephoned the New Jersey Treasury Department, Division of Taxation, in Trenton and asked to speak to state statistician Vijay Patel. After being transferred six times, he talked to a woman who said Patel had called in sick.

Watkins dialed Patel's home number.

"Hello," Mrs. Patel answered.

Watkins hung up without speaking.

Patel called back five minutes later. "Saw your name on Caller ID," he said, voice barely above a whisper. "I'm in the shed behind the house, calling on my cell phone."

Watkins was curious about how Mrs. Patel found out that Patel was at yesterday's game after he had told her he had to attend a business conference and left the house with a briefcase containing his cricket clothes and sneakers.

"One of our neighbors told her he saw me at the game," Patel related. "She didn't believe him. The sonofabitch drove her to the grounds."

It was said there was no such thing as a perfect crime. Watkins was ready to believe it.

"Is everything all right?" Watkins asked, feeling Patel's pain at the unraveling of the elaborate ruse, at the same time concerned that Patel might not be able to fulfill his responsibilities as the new club manager.

"She's still mad at me for what I did when she showed up at the game."

"You gestured to her that your cricket bat was your real wife," Watkins said, chuckling at the recollection despite the gravity of the fallout for Patel. "That wasn't nice."

"Yeah, but she embarrassed me by trying to make me leave the game, like I was a six-year-old kid," Patel said.

"Then you turned around and embarrassed her by your gesture."

"I stayed home from work to make it up to her, but she's still not talking to me," Patel said.

"Does that mean you wouldn't be able to take over for me as club manager this season?"

"I'll have to lie low for a while," Patel replied. "Say, I've got to go. She just came out of the house, looking for me."

Watkins sat back. Patel had a perfectly legitimate reason for copping out, but that didn't help the situation any.

Asking Gina for another reprieve so he could fight back against the establishment would be adding fuel to the fire. He really doubted their marriage would survive that conflagration. That meant he would have to maneuver behind her back. He hated the thought, but what option did Gina leave him? Simply walk away and let the club collapse? That wasn't an option. Even if he never played or watched another game, it was imperative that the club continue in perpetuity.

But it was more than that. Kruger had insulted them with that nasty crack about outsiders. In Kruger's eyes, they didn't count, and Mayor Quigley had sided with Kruger without even a courtesy call to the cricket club.

Who was this Quigley, anyway? As mayor, even though in an acting capacity, wasn't he supposed to represent everybody, especially the underdog? Instead, the man had shafted them, people he never met, on the say-so of an overgrown schoolyard bully who regarded them as "outsiders."

The situation couldn't stand. For him not to fight back would be contrary to his nature. Gina might not understand that, so he simply wouldn't tell her.

This was insane, Watkins thought. Just this morning he was professing his love for Gina and visualizing having a nervous breakdown if she left him because of his obsession for cricket, and now here he was thinking of deceiving her.

That didn't mean it couldn't be done. But with Patel as a failed example, he would just have to be inventive about how he went about his crime. As a former ad man and aspiring novelist, he should be able to come up with something original and foolproof.

His schedule today called for further editing of his manuscript, a murder-mystery set in a Philadelphia advertising agency. The story line went something like this: A Chicago firm buys the agency and shortly thereafter a top executive with the reputation of an ax wielder is sent by the new owners to trim the fat from their latest acquisition. Settling into his new Philadelphia digs with a large cup of black coffee, he tells the quivering staffers to come to him one by one with their resumes to reapply for their jobs. Before the day is over, he is found dead, facedown in his spilled coffee, a letter opener in his back. An aging account executive who didn't think he would survive the expected cuts, or adapt to the new culture if he did, is the chief suspect.

The story was an embellishment of his own situation. When his employer sold the ad agency, old-timers like him were offered an early-retirement package and he took it. Those who weren't there long enough to qualify for the package were asked to reapply for their jobs. With kids in college and house and car payments to be met, they had talked about ways to preempt the new CEO, permanently. The solution ranged from slipping arsenic in his pot of percolating coffee to putting a letter opener in the back.

In the novel, untitled so far, he was going for the more dramatic. If published, it would have the usual disclaimer. But he would have to put aside his writing chores for today.

Watkins dialed the leader of his writers' workshop that met the last Friday each month at the local coffeehouse. They chatted briefly about their respective novels before he asked, "Pam, do you mind calling me back at 5:30?"

The silence told him she was mystified. But not one to probe, Pam agreed.

Watkins returned to the backyard. Gina was on her knees, packing loose soil with her gloved hands around just-planted flowers.

"Get dressed," he said. "We're having a late lunch at your favorite Camden restaurant."

Her tears dried, but not too well. Gina regarded him with puzzlement.

"Come on, let's go," he said, swooping her up in his arms.

Gina shrieked in surprise, and for a moment they were back in Jamaica on their honeymoon and he was carrying her across the sand at the Ocho Rios beach into the crystal clear water.

His body still ached and it took an effort but he managed to deposit her safely on the deck.

"Go on," he said, patting her buttocks. "I'll put your tools away."

Gina stared at him, flabbergasted. It had been a while since he had lifted her like that and the playful gesture had produced the intended effect: She was smiling again.

******

From the outside, Cassandra's Soul Food Restaurant was your typical inner-city neighborhood eatery, with steel bars protecting the glass front, and heavy curtains behind the glass. The only clue that this wasn't another boarded-up building was the small neon sign in a corner of the window: "Open, Come In."

They had been here several times before, but it still took Watkins a while to figure out the entrance. There were no images of credit cards, menus, or dining reviews in the window.

The restaurant had seating for about thirty in two rooms. The buffet was still open. A TV blared from a stand against a wall that was blanketed with autographed pictures of actor Danny Glover of *Lethal Weapon* fame and other celebrities hamming it up with Cassandra and her employees.

The amiable Cassandra greeted them and made small talk while a waitress cleared a table among the half-dozen other diners.

They dined on beef oxtails and salmon croquettes, with side orders of collard greens, baked macaroni, and okra.

"Ready to tell me how your Avon meeting went?" Watkins said, as they shared a sweet potato pie for dessert.

"Amway," she said, slapping him playfully on the hand. "Amway products. You know what they are, don't you?"

"You really think you have what it takes to go around the neighborhood ringing doorbells?"

"It's not like the Avon lady calling," she said, slapping the other hand.

"Just kidding," he said. "I've seen the fancy brochures. It's all about organizing meetings in the home and inviting people over to buy Amway products."

"You don't mind, do you? You spend all your time writing; it gives me something to do."

"Of course I don't mind," Watkins said. "And you should do well, with all those women you've met over the years during your morning walks."

"That's what I'm thinking," she said. "A lot of them are seniors who prefer walking than going to the gym because those gym jocks make them feel their age."

"Sounds as though you have a solid client base."

"But I haven't made up my mind," she said.

"When do you think you will?"

"The Small Business Center at Rutgers University is holding a one-day seminar this week for people thinking of going into business," she said. "Mary and I will be going. I'll decide after the seminar whether I really want to do this. If I do decide, maybe you won't mind helping with the marketing."

"Whether it's Avon or Amway products, I'll be there for you," he assured her. "For the right commission, of course."

Yet another playful slap. "You said you went to visit Pops at the hospital. How was he?"

"No change."

"It must be hard on you."

"It is. Pops is my best friend."

"I know." She squeezed his hand, settled back, and laughed. "I remember that first time you two had that little bat-and-ball game."

He smiled at the recollection: the skating rink, he and Gina looking over the rails at their daughter, Maggie, little more than a toddler, who kept falling and getting up. Looking on from the other side was another black couple. The man eventually came over and introduced himself, Harold Richardson Minster. Watkins caught the Jamaican accent. Minster took them over to his wife, Wilhelmina. They pointed to a young child on the ice, Wilhelmina's niece.

Minster wanted to know what they were doing afterward. They were free, and Minster invited them over for snacks. While showing them the house, Minster displayed cricket gear he had brought with him from Ocho Rios, and soon they had a little bat-and-ball game going on in the yard. Minster lifted one of his lobs and shattered a kitchen window, scaring the bejesus out of their wives. The next weekend, they took their little game to a nearby schoolyard, and were joined by several immigrants who saw them while driving by; the nucleus of the Fernwood Cricket Club was created that day.

"We had a lot of good times, Pops and I," Watkins said, and heard the pain in his voice.

Her hand once again found his. "I did pray for him last night. He'll be all right."

Watkins looked into those big, dark-brown, still bewitching eyes and knew what she was thinking: This was the turning point of their lives; he had put his old ways behind him and begun now, with this meal, to put back into her life the spark that was missing. He hated himself at that moment. He was playing games when he should be coming clean.

He paid the bill. They chatted with Cassandra, and left.

Gina rubbed her stomach as they walked toward the wagon. "I think I just put back on two months of calories."

"You'll burn it off on your walk tomorrow morning. Then again, why wait? Let's see what's new in Mullica Hill."

The quaint village of Mullica Hill was a half-hour's drive away amid the farmlands of Gloucester County. For the next several hours, they browsed at the small shops and large cooperative-run barns that specialized in antiques and rare books. He bought her a reading lamp that caught her eye and that the dealer swore was the genuine object. He shelled out a hundred bucks, and she bought him a couple of limited-edition RCA Nipper porcelain dogs for his collection.

They capped the afternoon sharing a sundae at the Dairy Queen.

It was during that sharing, while thinking of Gina's plans to go into business for herself, that the answer to the cricket club's problems came like a lightning bolt to him.

Back home, he called Pierre from his basement office.

"I think we should buy that piece of property," he said excitedly. "Instead of a clubhouse, we build on it something that would be a cross between an exercise gym and a YMCA. It would have a swimming pool, sauna, treadmills and other exercise equipment. We market the facilities to seniors and have a steady stream of income."

Pierre was silent.

"What do you think?"

"It's ambitious," Pierre said.

Watkins waited for the "but."

"But there's already a YMCA in town along with at least a dozen private gyms, and they're all run by professionals," Pierre said. "What makes you think we can compete with them?"

Watkins had a ready answer: "Because we'll be going after an untapped market niche."

"And what niche is that?"

"The YMCA caters to families, and those private gyms to jocks," he told Pierre. "We'll be going after the seniors, particularly women who don't go to gyms because those jocks make them feel old and flabby. Based on all the reports on the aging of America, I think that's a market niche that's not being met. Of course, I'll have to do the research to back that up."

"You're talking about going into business..."

"I am," Watkins said. "We create a company in which the club members will be equal partners. I figure it would cost us two hundred grand to build the facility and for equipment."

"Two hundred grand in this market, and for equipment? That's way too low a figure."

"It's on the low side," Watkins agreed. "But we don't want to go in over our heads. We'll also be putting in our own sweat equity to keep the costs down. We finance the project, pay our bills and what's left over goes into our own pockets, or we use it to expand the business."

A longer silence, which told him this wasn't sitting well with Pierre.

"Well?"

"If I'm looking for additional investment income I may be better off investing in mutual funds."

Watkins didn't have a ready answer. He had been going on his emotions, thinking of Gina, and hadn't really thought it through. "What if I took the idea to a financial planner and he came up with a business plan that showed such a company can out-perform the stock market?"

"Then you'll have to take that business plan to a bank for financing because I don't have thousands of dollars lying around waiting for a good investment opportunity, and I doubt the others do," Pierre said. "And to get a business loan that size the bank would require us to put up some collateral. Angie's name is on the deed for our house, and I'll tell you right here and now she isn't going to sign anything."

"Maybe she will if she saw the cash-flow projections," Watkins said, let down that Pierre was putting up roadblocks instead of embracing the idea.

"Not only that," Pierre went on, "but you're talking about operating a business we know nothing about. We'd have to bring in professional managers, and they don't come cheap."

This, Watkins thought, was the easiest part of his proposal. "I already have a full-time CEO ready to take over."

"Yourself?" Pierre made a scoffing noise. "Your wife will kill you."

"She's the one I have in mind."

"Gina? Don't tell me this is all about setting up your wife in business."

"My wife keeps talking about starting her own business," Watkins said. "Her latest idea is selling Amway products.

That's nickel-and-dime stuff. If she's to go into business, why not something a lot more substantive?"

He got excited selling his candidate: Gina, he said, already had a base of potential clients among her group of morning walkers; she was good with numbers and with people; it would be a win-win situation, with Gina achieving her business goals, the club getting set for life with its own home grounds, and the whole thing paying off for everyone financially.

The silence was longer, deeper.

Watkins thought he had failed. He wished he had come up with something more definitive before broaching the subject to the normally business-minded Pierre.

"Before we take it to the members," Pierre finally said, "I suggest you get one of the experts to do the business plan. That way we know for sure whether we'd be sticking money down a rat hole."

Watkins heard Gina coming down the steps and ended his conversation with Pierre.

"It's Pam from your writers' group," Gina said, and handed him the cordless phone.

Pam wanted to know what was up.

"What time is the next group meeting?" he asked, loud enough for the retreating Gina to hear.

"The meeting at Don's place?" Pam asked, sounding perplexed. "That's not until next Friday, 6 o'clock."

"I'll try to make it," he said, hung up and called out to Gina to come get the phone back.

"Do you have a meeting of your writers' group?" Gina said, returning to accept it.

"Six o'clock," he said. "Want to come along?"

"I think I'll rest up from all this excitement."

Watkins settled back, thinking of financial planners from his days at the agency whom he could tap for some no-fee financial advice on his business idea. He had the means to invest in it and if the numbers showed it would be a profit maker, he should be able to sell it to club members. At least, the professionals among them who were stable, business-minded, and had good incomes.

As for Gina, it might be a tough sell, but she should be able to see it his way.

Watkins went upstairs and found Gina changing into house clothes.

He stood behind her and wrapped his arms around her waist.

"You'll be late for your meeting," she said, as he drew her closer.

"The meeting can wait," he said, and lifted her in his arms.

Gina shrieked even louder as he took her to the bed.

******

Maharaj Bhattacharya, aka Big Daddy to club members, lived with his two children and numerous extended family members in a three-story brick and stucco mansion on a wooded lot along Lilac Lane in the more affluent west side. Not bad, Watkins always thought, for a man who started out in The Fernwood Apartments walking to work at a gas station on the seedy boulevard, the main drag to Philadelphia, putting in sixteen-hour days for three years, parlaying his earnings into what would become a business empire, soon to include a chain of Indian fast-food restaurants.

His son, Surajit, showing no after-effects from the blow to the head from a well-hit ball he was fielding, and his sister, Jayati, greeted Watkins on the expansive veranda.

"Dad's out visiting some of his properties," said Jayati, and escorted him to the great room below-ground to a sea of guests sipping red and green liquids in tall glasses and nibbling finger food in decorative saucers.

Jayati formally announced Watkins' arrival and a tall, dark-haired man with a prune face who was conspicuously attired in a blue three-piece suit stepped out of the gathering, saucer in hand.

"Freddie Watkins!" he roared, extending a hand.

"Ahmed Siddique!" Watkins roared back, gripping the sticky hand. "Haven't seen you in a while. What are you up to these days?"

Siddique fished out a business card from his breast pocket. It identified him as Ahmed Siddique, investment banker.

"You used to be a nuclear engineer," Watkins remembered.

"People stopped building nuclear plants after TMI and Chernobyl," said Siddique, wiping dhal from his plate with puffed bread. "I'm helping Raj put a prospectus together for his IPO. He's going public."

"So he tells me."

"Heard you came out of retirement at the game yesterday to show the new guys you still have what it takes to win."

He sure did, Watkins thought. He mentally relived, in vivid Technicolor, the way he had lifted the ball over the head of the Jamaica Rebels pace bowler for the winning runs. It was a sweet shot.

"I got lucky," Watkins said, trying to be modest about it. "By the way, there's something you can do for us."

Watkins told him about the loss of the grounds and Sarubbi's suggestion that the club purchase land and develop it into an income-producing facility. He told Siddique the sort of facility he had in mind, a gym with all the usual amenities.

"It's a great idea," Siddique said.

"Financing it would be a problem," Watkins said. "The owner is asking for fifty grand for the land, and I figure it would cost us another two hundred grand for the facility."

"The banks got loads of money set aside for minority-owned businesses," Siddique said. "All you need to show them is a business plan that works and they're ready to shell it out."

"That's where you come in."

"Want me to help with a business plan? Be happy to. For the club, no charge."

Siddique had just said the magic words: *no charge.*

"Thanks."

"Let me put some numbers together and get back to you," Siddique said.

Jayati announced the arrival of Pierre, accompanied by a turbaned Bhupinder Singh, the club's newest recruit, who had set the foundation for yesterday's win against the Jamaica Rebels Cricket Club with a swashbuckling century. Singh was led like a blind man by his bulldog on a leash.

Siddique asked to be excused and made straight for Pierre and Singh.

Watkins spotted his neighbor, another recruit for yesterday's game, at the food bar.

"See you made it," he said to Michael Hankowsky.

"I wasn't sure I could get away from the TV station on time," Hankowsky said, sinking his teeth into a large cut of curried lamb, and ripping the meat off the bone like a starved wolf.

"Take your time," Watkins said, patting his neighbor on the shoulder and moving on to the only other white face among the gathering.

"Is your husband coming?" he asked Cindy Asquith.

"Shane's still upset at the way Napoleon belittled him at the game," Cindy said.

"Umpiring is a thankless job," Watkins said to the wife of the lone Englishman on the team.

"Shane would never intentionally cheat anybody out, especially his own teammates," Cindy said. "But give him time to cool off. In the meantime, I'll be his surrogate. Everything here sure looks good, doesn't it?"

Cindy used tongs to retrieve a doughnut-shaped object swimming in a bowl of white liquid and made room for it on her plate. "Oooh, look at this." The new object of her excitement was a green sauce. "Know what it is?"

Watkins confessed he didn't.

Cindy proceeded to decorate the food on her plate with generous scoops. "Ahh, now this is interesting..."

Cindy oohed and ahhed her way through the buffet and circled back. Watkins was full, but couldn't resist. He went for the tandoori chicken in a masala sauce, a little rice pudding, and the mango chutney.

Watkins circulated as he ate. Word of his heroics at yesterday's game had gotten out and the room buzzed as the guests recounted long forgotten nail-biting game endings similar to yesterday's, chatting in their native tongues and in English with such varied accents that it was apparent to Watkins, from the disconnected conversations and delayed laughter to intended jokes, that the West Indians didn't always understand what the East Indians and Pakistanis were saying and vice versa. But he thought this West-East disconnect mattered little. Cricket was their common language, the one thing inherited from their British colonizers and so innate in them as to transcend their religious, racial, ethnic and cultural differences.

"How often you guys do this?" Hankowsky said, after another trip to the buffet table. He lifted a chunk of curried goat with his fingers from his plate and stuffed it into his mouth.

"Not often enough," Watkins said.

Watkins felt something cold against his right hand and looked down into the pleading eyes of Singh's bulldog. Singh was holding court with a group of bearded, turbaned Sikhs. Getting no sympathy from Watkins, the dog proceeded to Cindy. The Englishman's wife took pity on the animal, going down on one knee, rubbing its neck and allowing it slurps off her plate.

Watkins was chatting with two other old-timers when he heard a loud crash at the food bar and saw that the dog had found the mother lode. Its front paws planted firmly on the table, the animal was lapping voraciously at the cream sauces. Singh screamed at the animal in Sikh and smacked its legs.

The dog retreated, smacking its lips.

A bell sounded and a hush fell over the room.

"Daddy has arrived," Jayati announced from the entrance.

Raj Bhattacharya, in a flannel shirt, silk scarf and jeans, made a grand entry. He worked the crowd with the air of a seasoned politician, squeezing hands and making quips on the way to a back wall. There, Bhattacharya turned to face the gathering and waited for silence.

"I trust you gentlemen, and ladies, have had a chance to renew acquaintances and to pass your cards around," Bhattacharya said. "It's a chance for you to do some networking. Just as we talked about in the old days. That's the way the white people do it. Old boys' network. Each one pulls the other up. No reason why we immigrants shouldn't."

A ripple of applause.

Watkins didn't join in. Could it be that Raj had invited them here to make a pitch for his IPO? No, that wouldn't qualify for the "big, big trouble" that Big Daddy had mentioned.

"But that's not the main reason I invited you here," Bhattacharya said, confirming Watkins' deduction. "If I told you in advance the real reason, you mightn't come."

"Don't tell me you're running for office," team captain Pierre quipped.

Louder applause.

"It's about time," said Siddique, the investment banker.

"I got a call this morning from a reporter at the Philadelphia Inquirer," Bhattacharya launched into his tale. "She said a man named Maximilian Kruger had faxed her a copy of a complaint he had just filed with the township police. According to the complaint, a bunch of illegals invaded the Little League grounds down at the George Washington Middle School yesterday. He wants the newspaper to do a story about it."

The audience groaned.

Watkins' anger soared. Not satisfied with getting them evicted from the middle school grounds, Max Kruger now was seeking to besmirch the cricket players in the media.

"I asked the reporter why was she calling me," Bhattacharya continued. "She said she spoke to this Indian chap at her paper who knows me personally. The chap told her that I was the club's financial backer. Now, when the lady reporter writes her story, how do you think she'll identify me?"

The question was addressed to no one, and to everyone. Bhattacharya searched the audience for answers.

Watkins took a stab at it. "As our chief corporate sponsor."

"Nope," Big Daddy said. "The reporter said she checked the paper's data base and my name's in there. Raj Bhattacharya, president of the South Jersey chapter of the New Jersey Indian Association. Operator of the 7-Eleven at the Circle, the Sunrise Motel on the boulevard, and a whole lot of other businesses. After speaking to this Kruger, she must be figuring I'm running some sort of criminal enterprise, using the Fernwood Cricket Club as a front to bring illegals into this country. So now, I'm the story."

A much louder groan.

"And if the police suspect I'm not on the up-and-up," Bhattacharya said, "the next thing you know U.S. immigration is knocking on my door to see if I'm harboring illegals. And once they come, the IRS won't be far behind. And before you can ask, 'Where is Big Daddy?' he's aboard an Air India flight in handcuffs."

Watkins thought that Bhattacharya had reason to be concerned, but that his fear of being the target of a criminal investigation was exaggerated. "Aren't you being paranoid?" he dared to ask.

"Paranoid!" Bhattacharya shrieked at him. "You heard about Mohiuddin? You think he was paranoid? They knocked on his door at the motel, and the next thing you know he has a one-way ticket to Calcutta, courtesy of the U.S. Immigration."

Watkins knew that Bhattacharya had told only half the story. What Bhattacharya should have explained was that the immigration agents had gone to Mohiuddin's motel to seek his assistance in rounding up so-called illegals who, the agents claimed, were moving into the area from Mexico and staying at cheap motels while looking for work at car washes and lawn-mowing and tree-cutting firms. But once the agents flashed their badges and announced, "Immigration!" Mohiuddin assumed they had come to check on his real motel records, not the one at the front desk, and began offering the agents a bribe to forget the whole thing. At least, that was the story told to Watkins, in confidence by Mohiuddin's former business partner, the said Raj Bhattacharya. And "that no-good Mohiuddin" who stole Raj's wife wasn't around to contradict it.

Watkins thought of a way to alleviate Bhattacharya's fear. "If you want, I'll call the reporter and let her know I'm the club's spokesman. That will take the heat off you."

"That would be helpful," Bhattacharya said. "Let's see if we can reach her before the newspaper starts printing."

Bhattacharya took him to a sitting room off the great room, made the call, and handed him the receiver. "Tell her I don't want my name in the papers. I had nothing to do with the game yesterday and I don't harbor illegals."

The reporter said her name was Erica Hobbs. She sounded rushed, as though on deadline with something much more important than cricket. Oh yes, she said, she had spoken to Mr. Bhattacharya. No, no, she wasn't about to rush into print the unsubstantiated allegations of Mr. Kruger, whom she knew, from her years of covering township meetings, as a man who threw his weight around. She was more interested in doing a story about cricket in Fernwood. She had seen the game during a trip to New Zealand and thought it was "kinda neat." She hadn't known that cricket also was played in Fernwood.

Hobbs said she would like to call him back later in the week and asked for his name and telephone number.

After a long pause, during which he decided that his helping Hobbs with her story posed no greater risk to his marriage than his presence here tonight, Watkins gave the reporter his full name and cell phone number.

Bhattacharya had his ear against the phone and overheard the exchange. "I don't want you to think anything bad," he said as Watkins hung up. "But a man of my position has to be careful. In this country, you know, people see us not doing too badly and they figure something fishy is going on, that we're getting government subsidy, really abusing the system. A bad press report about me, and people say, 'See that! What did I tell you?'"

Watkins assured the businessman that he understood, and they returned to the meeting. Bhattacharya made the announcement that everything had been straightened out.

Harry Sankar, the Trinidad psychologist, said, "Oh, good," and a collective sigh of relief swept over the room. Everyone thought well of Big Daddy. No one wanted to see him done in by the media and the U.S. Immigration.

Bhattacharya wasn't through. "I also want to talk about that team you put together yesterday," he said, addressing Watkins. "Based on what my son tells me, it wasn't the regular guys."

Watkins looked at Surajit. Young Bhattacharya made himself small in a corner.

"Don't blame the boy," Bhattacharya said. "He has good eyes. He sees things, but he wasn't spying for me."

Pierre, the titular club leader, said, "We were short. We thought we could put together a ragtag team."

"Ragtag!" Bhattacharya snapped. "Is that what we have become after twenty-five years?"

Watkins thought now might be an opportune time to let everyone know about the loss of their grounds. Pierre hadn't brought the subject up, no doubt leaving it to him. But he decided to hold off. No sense getting everybody riled up before the club had a chance to make its pitch to the Township Council.

"Who's this Napoleon Bonaparte fella anyway?" Bhattacharya was saying. "How come I've never heard about him?"

Pierre said, "Someone we picked up."

"My son tells me Napoleon went around threatening to shoot people," Bhattacharya said.

Watkins looked at Surajit, who slumped down in the corner.

"Napoleon called me up this morning and apologized," Pierre said.

"And who's Pretty Boy?"

"Someone else we picked up," Pierre said.

"Understand he has a roving eye," said Bhattacharya. "Was hitting on the ladies."

Watkins again looked at Surajit. The boy sought cover behind his sister.

"I'm disappointed in you guys," Bhattacharya said. "Really, I am. What happened yesterday was disgraceful. Really, really disgraceful. You let me down. Ragtags. Threats of shooting. Hitting on ladies. This is not the Fernwood Cricket Club I used to know."

Cindy Asquith raised her hand. Bhattacharya looked presidential as he recognized the Englishman's wife with a pointed finger.

"I'm a substitute teacher at Bishop Eustace," she said. "Come out to one of our field hockey games. You'll get an earful. All those nice, well brought up Catholic girls in the stands yelling, 'Break her legs! Break her legs!'"

"I appreciate what you're saying, but we aren't a bunch of girls," said Bhattacharya.

Hankowsky piped in, "You don't have to go to hockey games. Just pick up the papers or look at TV. Police called in to break up a fight at a wedding reception at the Coliseum. Over at Chuck E. Cheese, management evicted a group of six-year-olds celebrating a birthday party after they started a food fight."

"What's the point?" Bhattacharya asked Hankowsky.

"It all proves H. Rap Brown was right when he said violence is as American as cherry pie," Hankowsky said.

Cindy said, "I suppose it's difficult for you to live in this society and not become part of its culture of violence."

"You white people are accustomed to that kind of thing," Bhattacharya said to her. "Cricket is different. We are supposed to represent the highest ideals of sportsmanship. We are the top echelon."

Watkins listened for the next several minutes as Bhattacharya held court, extolling the high ideals of the game, like a politician running for office on a platform of morality. He resisted the temptation to interrupt with a defense of their actions. Bhattacharya, after all, was their money man. The least he could do was let the businessman vent.

Watkins thought it time to slip away. He had solved Bhattacharya's "big, big" problem, enjoyed meeting the club's alumni and didn't think he should push it with Gina by hanging around. Maybe he could get in an hour or two of writing before retiring to bed. Better yet, end the perfect day for Gina by popping that bottle of wine in the refrigerator, digging out the old vinyl and dancing in the dark to "Unforgettable."

"Gentlemen! Gentlemen!" Bhattacharya called to order as the meeting spun out of control.

Watkins felt a tap on his shoulder.

"Before you go, let's say a prayer for Pops." Pierre held his hand, and asked the others to hold hands and to bow their heads in silent prayer, each in his own religion, for Pops' speedy recovery.

A loud, lapping sound broke the silence. Watkins traced it to the buffet table. The bulldog had seized the moment. His front legs were back up on the other end of the table and he was having another go at the fresh bowls of cream sauces.

Singh, shouting in his native tongue, forced his way through to the table, grabbed at the leash and yanked. The dog's nails, embedded in the tablecloth, dragged it down.

Watkins jumped back as the utensils, food, fruits and drinks spilled across the Persian rugs.

CHAPTER 2

Tuesday, May 1, the following day.

Watkins awoke around 8 to the aroma of coffee, and the sound of Gina's humming "Unforgettable" along with Nat King Cole and daughter Natalie on the radio. He had arrived home from the meeting at Bhattacharya's place shortly before 9 to find his wife still high on their impromptu day's outing climaxed by their passionate lovemaking. She had waited up for him, and they ended the night on a much higher note, consuming half the bottle of wine that she had chilled and rough-housing on the rug.

He heard the doorbell ring, followed by the sound of women's voices. The door closed. The voices ceased.

Watkins dragged himself to the bedroom window in time to see Gina and neighbors Mary Hankowsky and Carmen Alvarez pile into Alvarez's van and drive off. Having stayed at home to raise children who were now all adults and had left home, the women believed this was their time to enjoy life. If today were like any other day, they would spend an hour or so taking their power walk along the lake, then would have a hearty, low-calorie breakfast at some new diner. Later, they might visit a retail outlet that was having a closeout or grand-opening sale. If, perchance, he wasn't in when Gina returned, she eventually would ask whether he noticed anything different about the house. On close scrutiny, he would discover that a piece of furniture, a picture, a plant, or a piece of porcelain, or some strange artifact, had joined the Watkins family. Gina would wax warm about what a great buy it was and he would say yes, it looks nice, and it would sit there for a few months; then, like the curator at a museum, she would ease it to the storage room to make space for a new piece.

Watkins didn't have a problem with his wife's routine. Gina was happy with it, and it spared his having to wake up faster than he was able to after writing late into the night.

Over coffee, with scrambled eggs, bacon and toast, which Gina had prepared and left for him in the microwave oven, Watkins wondered how he would swing tonight's Township Council meeting.

Two nights out in a row was likely to arouse suspicion, especially if tonight's meeting ran late.

The answer came while he was in the shower.

He telephoned Michael Hankowsky at his job at TV-8 in Philadelphia.

"I need a reason to get out of the house so I can attend tonight's township meeting," he said. "How about if you call me when Gina gets back and invite me to one of your photo exhibits in Philadelphia?"

"Is that the best you can do for an alibi?" the cameraman replied with a chuckle. "Let me handle this."

"What do you have in mind?"

"Just leave it to me," Hankowsky said. "I'll go with you to the meeting, and I'll bring Timmy along. The cricket club needs all the support it can get."

Gina returned mid-afternoon with a wooden stepladder that doubled as a chair. She explained that she and her girlfriends got lost on the way to Lenox China near Trenton but found this little furniture warehouse. The stepladder was just what she wanted to be able to reach items on the top pantry shelf. Now she didn't have to bother him to reach up for the items. He agreed that it was practical.

Gina sat on the edge of his desk. "After beating up on you for spending so much time with the boys, I know I shouldn't be asking this. But would you mind if I went out with the girls this evening?"

The question startled him.

"I shouldn't have mentioned it," she said, observing his reaction.

"No, no," Watkins said, thinking that the gods surely were on his side. "Please, after putting up with me, you deserve a night out with the girls."

"Carmen happens to mention that it's been twenty-five years since we began our morning walks. Mary thought it calls for a celebration."

"As long as it's not a visit to one of those raunchy, male striptease joints, I'm all for it."

"Actually," she said, with sudden girlishness, "Carmen did suggest we do something wild."

"I think it's time Mrs. Alvarez found herself a new boyfriend."

"Oh, didn't I tell you about the postman? He's been dropping her off more than the mail. Yesterday, it was a box of Godiva chocolate. That's all she needs to get her weight back up."

Gina prattled on with the latest in the saga of her fellow walkers, from the state of their marriages and love lives to their health, providing Watkins with fodder for his next book. It, too, would contain the usual disclaimer.

Gina left the house at 6:50 for dinner with the girls.

Hankowsky called at 7. "Guess who planted the idea of a girls' night out?"

"You did?" Watkins shouldn't have been surprised. Like him, Hankowsky had a creative mind.

"Our wives might have been a bit wary about my inviting you to a photo exhibit at such short notice," Hankowsky said. "I suggested the girls' night out to Mary instead, and she ran with it to Gina and Mrs. Alvarez."

"You're a genius."

"Like I said, anything for cricket," Hankowsky said.

******

Watkins circled the township administrative complex several times before he found a parking space. On the way in, he ran into the Hankowskys. Timmy was lugging his father's TV camera. They, too, had been circling.

"Must be something big going on," said Hankowsky, who had parked alongside a KYW-Eyewitness News TV truck. "Is Cindy Asquith coming?"

"Why? You've got the hots for the Englishman's wife?" Watkins said, and saw Timmy smile. "Sorry, kid."

"You're mostly people of color fighting a white establishment," Hankowsky said. "It wouldn't hurt to have at least one white woman standing in back of you."

"Next time I'll have to remember to invite Cindy," Watkins said, and turned to Timmy. "What's with the camera?"

"This is Dad's idea," Timmy said.

"We'll be using it as a psychological weapon," Hankowsky explained. "Council members are less likely to steamroll over the cricket club if they know they're on camera."

"Just make sure I'm not in the picture," Watkins warned the Hankowskys.

The council chamber seated two hundred. The place was crammed. Peering in from the doorway, Watkins saw a woman speaking into a microphone on the edge of the audience, her face bathed in television klieg lights. She was addressing the seven council members. They were six men in suits and a woman in a Cleopatra hairstyle and John Lennon circle-rimmed glasses. The council members sat behind nametags on a long table on a stage.

There was a nametag for Neil Quigley but the mayor's chair was vacant.

Scanning the audience, Watkins spotted Max Kruger and son Otto in their Fernwood Little League sweatshirts, surrounded by about forty youngsters in baseball uniforms. He also spotted club president Pierre, standing against the back wall. He wore a business suit and looked every bit the high-priced lawyer he wasn't.

Watkins was making his way, with Hankowsky and son behind him, toward Pierre when a rail-thin man pressed a flier into his hands. Watkins recognized him as a community activist from the township's grassroots Fair Housing Council. He had become a fixture on local cable TV, forever railing about Fernwood's unwillingness to provide affordable housing for the poor.

The missive read: *Who - Fair Housing Council; What - Rally; When - 11 a.m. Wednesday, May 2; Where - Steps of City Hall, Camden; Why - the circumvention by the Township Council of the spirit and intent of the affordable-housing law.*

Pierre created space for them along the wall, and whispered, "Final public hearing on the affordable-housing resolution. It's the only item on the agenda. When they're through the meeting will be open to the public. That's when we lodge our complaint to council."

"I see our friend Max Kruger is here," Watkins said.

"I suspect someone alerted him we were coming and he came with his little army to challenge us," Pierre said. "We'll have to be forceful."

"Who else from the club is coming?" Watkins asked, looking around for others.

"That's it; you and me and the Hankowskys," Pierre said.

Watkins had expected at least a half-dozen members to show up, but was more disappointed than surprised by the poor turnout.

Watkins turned his attention to the woman at the microphone. She was blasting the resolution, which was supposed to bring closure to a two-decade-old state edict to Fernwood to provide affordable housing. The issue had dominated the news since late last year when the mayor of Fernwood told a Chamber of Commerce business luncheon that Fernwood would build such housing "over my dead body."

Rumors of the remark, intended to be private among business associates, were so widespread that the media reported them. At first, the mayor vehemently denied making the statement. An audio tape of the remark was aired on the news, along with his denial, and the fair housing activists said the mayor had lost his credibility and should step down permanently. The mayor, ironically, obliged by having a fatal heart attack, prompting the June 12 election to fill the remaining two years of his four-year term.

Under the proposal being debated, the township would fulfill its obligation under the state mandate by building the required housing in nearby Camden, one of the poorest cities in America. The township also would donate a million dollars to Camden. The woman at the mike was accusing the council of circumventing the law and conspiring with the mayor of Camden to keep poor Camden residents, the likely pool of candidates for the new housing, from moving into Fernwood.

"I wouldn't be surprised," she said, "if members of Township Council bribed the mayor of Camden to accept the deal."

That remark drew lusty applause from the front rows, and a yawn from the council president. The man then looked at his watch, told the speaker that her three minutes had expired, and banged his gavel when she tried to continue. The woman raised her voice, and he banged louder. She gave up and sat in the front row.

A vote was taken and the measure passed, six to one, with Andrea Grimes voting against. Reporters rushed out into the corridor, along with most of the audience. The reporters besieged the rail-thin man, seeking his reaction to the vote.

"It ain't over yet," Watkins heard him say above the commotion.

Council President Cecil Blair directed a council staff member to shut the door, and announced that the meeting was now open to non-agenda matters.

Watkins felt Pierre's elbow in his ribs. "This is your show," Pierre said.

Watkins hesitated. He had come to the meeting casually dressed and it occurred to him now that the majority on council, the men in suits, might more easily relate to the nattily attired Pierre.

"Go on," Pierre said, with another jab.

Watkins stepped up to the mike.

"Okay, young man," Blair addressed him. "What's your beef?"

Conscious of Timmy near the door, with the camera focused on him, Watkins gave his name and address and said he was a representative of the Fernwood Cricket Club.

"I wasn't aware we had a croquet club in Fernwood," Blair said.

"Cricket."

"So, how can we help you?"

Watkins proceeded to describe the club's founding a quarter-century ago. The township had lots of open space then and Joseph Sarubbi helped the cricket club pick a spot off Gardenia, and the spot became known as The Cricket Field. He recounted what the council members already knew, how the council decided last year to expand The Cricket Field into a full park, to be called Fernwood Park. Along with a wicket for cricket, it was to include ball fields for other sports.

"Mr. Sarubbi, the recreation director, assigned us to the George Washington Middle School grounds until the park reopened," Watkins continued. "We discovered yesterday that the mayor had reassigned the grounds exclusively to Little League. That means we have no place to play."

"Unfortunately, Mr. Quigley had a death in the family last night," said Blair. "He might be away for the next couple of weeks."

"We can't wait that long," Watkins said. "We have a number of home games to play before the park reopens."

Blair looked out into the audience. "I see Maximilian Kruger is here with us. Max, can you work out something with the croquet club?"

Kruger stood. "Hell no!"

Blair cleared his throat. "I guess you can't work it out among yourselves. Why don't we take this up in caucus after our public session."

Watkins glared at Kruger as he rejoined Pierre. The man definitely had come angling for a fight.

The two other complainants went quickly.

One, a Mrs. Jones from the township's Woodland section, asked why green moss was forming inside her bedroom closets and her clothes were "getting moldy."

The council president explained that her home was built on an illegal dump. He suggested she might want to add her name to a class-action suit that had been filed against the developer.

The second, a Mr. Rupert from Magnolia Gardens, gave the Township Council an ultimatum: Get rid of the softball field near his house or he would sue to force its removal and seek compensation for a slew of broken windows from wayward balls.

Blair asked Mr. Rupert whether he would be satisfied

if the Softball Association relocated its diamond to face the opposite direction. It used to be that way, Rupert said, but was turned around after batters complained about sun in their eyes. Blair promised to look into it, referring to the complaint, not the sun.

With no further business, the council adjourned to the caucus room at back. Grimes rushed down from the stage to press business cards and campaign buttons into every hand she could find.

The caucus chamber was a large conference room with a rectangular table that took up most of the space.

Blair sat at the head of the table. Kruger and son stood behind Blair, with his army of Little Leaguers lining the back and side walls.

Watkins sat at the other end of the table facing Blair and the Krugers. Pierre sat next to him. The Hankowskys stood behind them like bodyguards.

Pierre handed Blair his business card and told the council president the cricket club wanted a live recording of the meeting.

Blair read the card and said, "Spoken like a lawyer gathering evidence for a lawsuit. Caucuses are public meetings and cameras are allowed, but you'd be amazed by the amount of work that can get done outside the glare of cameras."

Pierre asked Watkins what he thought, and Watkins deferred to the elder Hankowsky, who nodded at his son. Timmy shut off the camera.

Blair said to Timmy, "I watched you hit that turn-around jump-shot to beat the buzzer and win the game for Rutgers last Friday. That was quite a shot."

"Thanks," Timmy said.

"You've taken up cricket now?"

"Mr. Watkins is our neighbor," Timmy said.

"So," Blair said to Watkins, "how can we help you people?"

Watkins objected to the presence of Kruger and his group. Blair repeated that caucuses were public meetings; anyone could sit in.

"You people are in America now," Otto Kruger interjected. "Why don't you play an American sport?"

"Cricket is an American sport," Hankowsky said.

"Bull!" Maximilian Kruger said. "We've been playing baseball in this country for more than a hundred and fifty years."

Hankowsky said, "Cricket has been played in England since the Middle Ages, to Pope Gregory IX."

Watkins cringed as Hankowsky, eager to show off his newfound book knowledge, went into a diatribe about how Abe Lincoln once played cricket. So did American soldiers at Valley Forge during lulls in the Revolutionary War. The inference was that the game helped George Washington's army relieve stress and tension, and, when time came to take up the musket, made them a better fighting force for they did win the war, though never fully mastering the fundamentals of the cricket. That's why they changed the rules and called it baseball.

The elder Kruger was breathing fire by the time Hankowsky was through. "What are you saying, that Abner Doubleday didn't invent baseball?"

"Papa Doubleday," said Hankowsky, "took a six-hour game, changed some of the rules to fit the American two-hour attention span, and called it baseball."

Otto Kruger said, "Man, you got some mouth!"

"Look it up," Hankowsky said.

Max Kruger said to the council members, "Did you hear what he just said? Good as accused Papa Doubleday of being a plagiarist. Better watch this guy."

Watkins said, "He's right. Cricket is a return to our roots."

"Our roots!" Max Kruger said.

"What do you mean by *our*?" Otto said.

"Thanks for the enlightenment," Blair said to Watkins. "But let's move on. Our mayor would have had his reason for reassigning the George Washington Middle School grounds to the Little League exclusively. It would be inappropriate for us to telephone him at this time to get his input. So, I suppose we'll just have to find another temporary ground for cricket."

"No, you won't!" Max Kruger said. "There aren't enough grounds in this town for our people."

Pierre said, "Who's calling the shots here?"

"I'm in charge," the council president said to Pierre. "Everyone, please address your remarks to the chair."

"The first obligation," Kruger said to Blair, "is to our residents, our taxpayers."

"And that doesn't include us?" Watkins asked Kruger. His blood had started to boil.

"If you are taxpayers, prove it," Max Kruger said.

Pierre said, "You're the one making the inference that we are outsiders: The onus is on you to supply the proof."

"We don't have to prove anything," said Otto Kruger.

"I'll do the talking," the elder Kruger said to his son, and Otto sulked. "My son's correct," he added, addressing Watkins. "As Americans, we don't have to prove anything; you do."

Hankowsky said to Max Kruger, "And when did you become an American, Herr Kruger?"

Blair pounded a gavel. "We are here to solve a problem, not exacerbate it. Please, gentlemen, let's proceed with that in mind."

"Let's have their names; we'll check it against our tax rolls," Kruger said.

"Max has raised the question of residency," Blair said, and craned his neck to address Kruger behind him. "Am I to take it, Max, that if you're satisfied that these people..."

"These people have names," Hankowsky said.

"...are tax-paying township residents," Blair continued, raising his voice, "you'll drop your opposition to the cricket club, and might be willing to work out an accommodation with them?"

"I might," said Kruger, with the smug look of a man who held all the cards.

"Well then," Blair said, turning back to address Watkins, "that shouldn't be a problem for you people."

"His name is Freddie Watkins," Hankowsky said.

"Would that be a problem, Mr. Freddie Watkins?" Blair rephrased his remark.

"I thought you said you're the one calling the shots," Watkins shot back.

"You're right," said Blair. "Forget about Max. I am asking the question. Do you people live here?"

Watkins said, "Does Max Kruger live here? Do the members of Little League live here? Or the football, or baseball, or softball players?"

"Unfortunately," Blair said, "those teams aren't the ones before us tonight."

"He can't answer the question," Kruger said. "I suspect they're all out-of-towners crossing the border from Camden to monopolize our fields."

Hankowsky said, "On what basis do you assume they're out-of-towners from Camden? Because they are people of color?"

Blair banged his gavel harder. "Let me ask the question," he said to Watkins. "Do you people live here?"

Watkins didn't like where they were headed. They had come seeking redress to a grievance, but had been put on the defensive. Kruger was in control. "Some do, and some don't," he answered, with reluctance.

"How many do, and how many don't?"

"That," Watkins said, "all depends on the makeup of the team on a particular day, particular month, particular year. Some days we all live here, some days some do and some don't."

"I'm confused," said Blair.

Pierre said, "The club is open to everyone, regardless of residency. We made this clear to the township from the very beginning. Our members come and go throughout the season. That's no different from any other amateur sporting group."

"What I understand you to be saying," Blair said, "is that you may start the season with one set of players and end up with a different set of players."

"Correct," Watkins said.

Kruger said, "And how long does your game last?"

"I'll ask the questions," Blair told Kruger. "How long does the game last?"

"We play mostly weekend games," Watkins said. "The games starts at 1 and go until 6:30, 7 o'clock."

"And how many players comprise your team?" Blair continued to probe.

"Eleven players make up a team," Watkins answered.

"That means," Blair reckoned, "that in any given match, you have eleven players, some of whom may or may not live in the township, tying up our fields for an entire afternoon, while our kids have no place to play?"

"There you go," Kruger said, raising both hands like a cricket umpire signaling six runs. "Couldn't have said it better myself. They've got eleven people. We got two thousand members."

"And each has two parents," Watkins said. "And that's four thousand votes that you've promised to the mayor."

"Hey, you," Kruger said, advancing. "Watch your face!"

"Get back, Max," Blair said.

Kruger growled, and retreated.

Councilwoman Grimes spoke for the first time: "Max, I trust the Little League and its purported two thousand members can stand up to similar scrutiny."

"Go ahead," Kruger dared Grimes, "check on us."

Grimes said, "Believe me, Max, you don't want to open that Pandora's box."

"Stop politicking," Blair rebuked Grimes.

Grimes turned to Watkins. "I imagine that the club is more than eleven players."

"A lot more," Watkins agreed.

"How many members would you say you have altogether?"

Watkins estimated the club had up to fifty dues-paying members, plus half that many associate members.

"And you do have your supporters, of course?" she said, lobbing another easy one.

Watkins saw where she was guiding him, like a defense lawyer leading a witness, and he took her there: "Several hundred supporters, plus our wives, girlfriends and friends and neighbors."

"All U.S. citizens, I'd imagine," said Grimes. "And registered to vote."

"We take our voting privileges seriously," said Watkins, in no position to give the councilwoman the information she wanted.

Grimes pushed her chair back, the better to address council president Blair. "A question for you, Mr. President: Can this township legally give the Little League, a private organization, exclusive rights to use public fields at the expense of other taxpayers, particularly the cricket club, given its long history in this town?"

Kruger again stepped forward, snarling, "*Wenn die Kricketspieler nicht gleich abhauen, kriegen Sie etwas*, you ugly bitch."

A hush fell over the room.

Grimes stared, with reddening face, at Kruger.

Blair again cleared his throat. "Max is free to express his views. That he certainly did. I just wish he would refrain from name calling."

Watkins expected the council members to demand an apology from Kruger, and when that didn't appear likely, said, "The councilwoman asked a legitimate question. Can you, members of council, give exclusive rights to a private organization to use public fields at our expense? We'd like an answer."

Blair glanced at the wall clock, then the corridor. "It's getting late, and I see there are others waiting to air their grievances. We will take the matter under advisement. In the meantime, to aid our deliberations, I suggest to you, Mr. Watkins, that you provide me with the names, addresses and telephone numbers of your members."

Pierre said, "Will Kruger be doing the same with respect to the Little League?"

"He will not be," said Blair. "At least, not at this time."

Hankowsky said, "I think we know what your answer will be."

"And just how do you know what our answer will be?" Blair challenged Hankowsky.

The TV cameraman said, "I've listened to this discussion, and Max Kruger's earlier reference to outsiders. Mr. Watkins, who, as my son pointed out, is my neighbor, asked Kruger how he determined they are from Camden. He didn't answer the question."

"Mr. Kruger is not required to respond to Mr. Watkins' question," Blair said.

"Funny, but it's the same argument we used to get rid of our basketball courts," Hankowsky said.

"What are you insinuating?" Blair said.

Hankowsky said, "We used to have basketball courts at all our fields. A few years ago we cut those hoops down and built tennis courts."

Blair said, "We did have complaints that non-taxpayers were coming in from across the border to monopolize our basketball courts and our kids couldn't get to play."

"We called them outsiders," said Hankowsky. "Same code word Kruger keeps using. It was a very polite way of saying they aren't white, they aren't like us."

It was Blair's turn to change color. "You aren't calling us racists, are you? Because if you are, just look around this town. Why, we are a regular United Nations. We are a model of diversity and affirmative action."

"If we are," said Hankowsky, "how come I see nothing but lily white faces in every township department, including the Police Department?"

"You are calling us racists!" Blair said.

"I go back to the original question," Hankowsky said. "How does Max Kruger know they are from Camden? I believe the first time he met and talked to Mr. Watkins was at our cricket game on Sunday, when he called the cops and demanded that they kick us off the grounds."

Kruger jabbed a finger at Hankowsky and said. "I thought I recognized you!"

"Talk about being clairvoyant," Hankowsky said, ignoring him. "Merely by looking at them, Kruger determined that the cricket players or any person of color, for that matter, had to be outsiders, non-taxpayers, an invasion from Camden. Without having spoken so much as a word to them! No different than the basketball players!"

Timmy said, "Most of those so-called non-taxpayers monopolizing the basketball courts were my African American friends from The Fernwood Apartments right here in Fernwood."

"And how would you know that, Timmy?" Blair said.

"Because," Timmy said, "back in high school a group of us used to leave the school gym and go down to the courts at The Fernwood Apartments to practice against them. They were good competition for us. That three-point, turnaround jump shot that won that last game for Rutgers, who do you think taught me that shot?"

"Well," Blair drawled, loosening his tie, and hemming and hawing, "that was real nice of them." He looked toward the hallway. "Will the next group come in?"

CHAPTER 3

Wednesday, May 2

From the front door, Watkins waved to Gina and Mary as they drove off in Mary's Hyundai. Instead of taking their normal power walk, the women were headed to a seminar for would-be entrepreneurs at the Small Business Center at Rutgers University.

Once the vehicle was out of sight, Watkins retreated to his basement office to plan his next move. The Township Council president essentially had established two sets of rules for use of township playgrounds: one for the non-cricket clubs, and the other with a much higher bar, over which Fernwood Cricket Club was being asked to jump.

He compiled the requested membership list.

At 9, a half-hour later, he drove over to the municipal building and handed the township clerk the list, with copies for the members of the council.

Watkins then walked over to the Office of Community Recreation.

"Heard from my sources on council that Max Kruger was really smoking last night," Joseph Sarubbi greeted him.

"That's putting it mildly," Watkins said, and gave the recreation director a copy of the membership list.

Sarubbi studied the list. "Are all the people listed here immigrants?"

"I thought you said nationality wasn't the main issue."

"It isn't, but you can't ignore it," Sarubbi said. The telephone rang. He let it ring. "You have to be realistic. Right now, cricket is perceived to be an immigrant sport. You should take a page from the soccer moms. Make it an American sport."

"It is an American sport."

"You're talking ancient history here, Partner," said Sarubbi. "Right now the typical American couldn't tell you the difference between cricket and a hole in the ground. I used to be that way, remember?"

How Watkins remembered!

Sarubbi finally picked up the phone. It was the superintendent of schools. The two men talked about a softball field, a mansion, broken windows and a threat of a lawsuit.

Watkins thought the dispute sounded familiar.

Sarubbi agreed to a 5 o'clock meeting at the field with the superintendent and the homeowner.

Watkins waited for him to hang up, and drew Sarubbi's attention to the two Hankowskys on the list. "They're native born."

"It's a start," Sarubbi said. "But I'm talking more about the youth of Fernwood. The mayor says he wants to give the youth priority. Well, start a youth league. As I said, do what the soccer moms did. Go after the kids. Bring them on board and you'll get the parents in your corner. You do that, you cut Max Kruger off at the knees with the same sword he's holding over the mayor's head."

Watkins liked the idea, but thought it a bit grandiose. "All we want is our own little patch of green."

"You're limiting your sights," Sarubbi said. "That's not the American way. This country thinks big. We've got to be bigger and better than the next guy. Think big, and you know what?"

"What?"

"A youth team could serve as your farm team. Kids do grow up. Catch them now and by the time they're ready to leave school you've got a lot of young blood for your adult team."

Sarubbi was making sense. Still....

"What would you say is the average age of your club members?" Sarubbi said.

Watkins figured forty, more likely forty-five.

"And what's your record like?"

"We play for fun," Watkins said.

"That means you don't win. You used to work in advertising and public relations, right? You know about the value of PR. A youth league not only would be good PR and provide you with new blood, it also can help improve your record and you wouldn't have to play for fun anymore. You can play to win."

Everything Sarubbi said made sense, and the thought excited Watkins But just how would he go about recruiting American-born youths? He had an image of himself standing outside the fence at a soccer game, stopping kids as they went on and came off the field, asking their names, addresses and telephone numbers. Suspicious parents rush over. "Who was that man?" they ask the kids. "What was he saying to you? Somebody, please, call the police."

Sarubbi was back on the phone. This time the school superintendent wanted him to handle a complaint from neighbors about noise from a baseball broadcast booth down at Field No. 10.

He put the phone down. "This is how I spend most of my day. In the big cities, people worry about life-and-death issues. Crime. Poverty. Dirty streets. Here in Fernwood, we worry about the geese mucking up our lakes and ponds, about kids not getting enough playing time at ball fields, and, talk about bureaucratic overreach, about not keeping our lawn grass to regulation height! Where were we?"

"How do I go about recruiting members for a youth league?"

Sarubbi summoned his secretary with a shout.

"I want you to send out a notice to the parents of all middle-schoolers stating that the cricket club is starting a cricket league for the kids," Sarubbi instructed her. "For further information they're to contact this office. Send it out ASAP so the kids can take it home after school today. And remind me to clear it with the school superintendent." Sarubbi turned to Watkins. "How's that?"

Once again, Sarubbi had proven himself a friend of the cricket club. "Thanks," Watkins said, "but I suspect that many of those kids you're asking us to recruit already play Little League and their parents are among the four thousand votes that Max Kruger is holding over the mayor's head."

"Most likely," Sarubbi conceded. "But many of those parents also will be soccer moms who represent a much bigger voting bloc. They are more likely to be more receptive to their kids taking up another foreign sport."

Sarubbi gave him the number for the Fernwood Soccer Association president. "You might want to follow up by giving her a call," he added. "Sit down with the moms. Let them see your face, hear your voice. Sell yourself and your game. Get them to sign a petition demanding a playing field for kids' cricket. As the ones who will be teaching them cricket, your members should have access to the field, too. Present that petition to Quigley when he returns from his bereavement. He sees those signatures and he sees votes. That's what it comes down to: votes in the upcoming mayoral elections."

It was a course of action Watkins was more than willing, and ready, to undertake. But he recognized that he couldn't embark on such a mission without word eventually getting back to Gina. Asking Pierre and the other club members to create an alliance with the soccer moms as a way to get their patch of green to play the game of the youth would be a waste of time.

"I'll see what I can do," Watkins said, leaving open the possibility of his active involvement.

"Let me know how you make out," Sarubbi said, grabbing his jacket off the back of the chair. "In the meantime there's also the land-purchase option."

"I should have an answer on that for you soon."

******

69

Back in the wagon, Watkins flipped open his cell and dialed Pierre's law office.

Pierre, his secretary said, had left for court with a fellow cricketer: Bhupinder Singh.

Watkins recalled that part of the reason Singh showed up at the weekend game was to talk to Pierre about representing him a shooting incident. He didn't know that Pierre had agreed to take on the case.

"What court and what time is the hearing?" he asked.

"It's scheduled for 11 a.m. before Judge Malcolm King, Courtroom 202-B, Camden County Courthouse on Market Street in Camden."

******

The affordable-housing activists had kept good their promise of a rally on the steps of Camden City Hall. About sixty people marched in a circle, holding up caricatures, with potentially libelous accusations, of the mayor of Camden.

The president of the Fair Housing Council stood at a microphone at the top of the steps, vowing to fight the planned transfer of Fernwood's affordable-housing obligation to Camden all the way to the Supreme Court.

Inside, the corridor near Courtroom 202-B floor was crowded with men in turbans. Singh was one of them. He was talking to Pierre. Both wore suits.

Watkins was winding his way toward the two men when a courtroom door was pushed open and a marshal appeared in the doorway.

"Singh!" the marshal shouted.

A sea of turbans swirled toward him.

"Whoa! Whoa! Whoa!" the marshal cried, motioning them with both hands to halt. "Which one of you is Singh?"

They were all Singhs.

The marshal stuck his head back into the courtroom, asked the clerk for a first name, then shouted for Bhupinder Singh.

"That's us," Pierre said to his client.

Lawyer and client went in. Watkins followed.

The judge raised a face that was all jowls topped with golden locks and peered at Singh, now at the defense table with his attorney. "What do we have here?" the judge said, and consulted his files. "Assault with a potentially lethal weapon, to wit, a cricket bat."

The prosecutor, a young man who looked to be barely out of law school, told the judge that the defendant was now represented by counsel, Emile Pierre, and on the advice of counsel had decided to plead guilty to the charge.

The judge seemed to grow taller in his chair. "Let's hear the facts of the case."

Four rows back in the crowded room, Watkins leaned forward to hear the facts, as narrated by the prosecutor: *The incident occurred during an attempted holdup of Singh's gas station. As two ski-mask wearing, pellet-gun toting gunmen were rifling the office safe, Singh whipped out the cricket bat that he carried around for protection, and began whacking away. The gunmen were rescued by the police, who happened to be driving by. The gunmen were charged with attempted robbery and possession of unlicensed firearms. Singh was charged with using excessive force because he allegedly continued to beat the gunmen when they no longer posed a threat to him. While they were interviewing him, the cops asked Singh why was he bleeding. Only then did Singh realize that he had been shot in the chest. The pellet wounds weren't life threatening.*

"May I see the weapon in question?" the judge asked the prosecutor when he was through with his narration.

The prosecutor held up a heavy, long-handled cricket bat, labeled *Exhibit-A.*

"May I hold it?"

The prosecutor handed the willow to the court clerk who handed it to the judge, who inspected the physical evidence, front and back, said, "Rather unique weapon," and gave it back to the clerk who returned it to the prosecutor.

The prosecutor explained that as part of a plea, the prosecutor was recommending six months of probation, with some community service.

The judge asked Pierre whether he had anything to add to what the prosecutor had said.

Pierre described Singh as a hard-working immigrant who had armed himself with the bat after being robbed several times.

"My client," he added, "is a man of good character. I have a witness who can vouch for him."

Pierre looked around at Watkins and motioned for him to get up.

Character witness? *I met the guy over the weekend pumping gas and invited him to the game; that's the extent of my knowledge of Bhupinder Singh,* Watkins thought.

"That's not necessary," the judge said and shifted his gaze to Singh. "Do you wish to say anything?"

Singh, standing with his hands straight down at his sides and his chest out like a prisoner at the wall awaiting the firing squad, said he had nothing to say.

"Six months' probation, plus one hundred hours of community service," the judge said, writing the entry in his book. He looked down on Singh. "Instead of a cricket bat, you might want to get yourself a dog."

"He already has gotten himself a bulldog," Pierre said.

So that's how Bhupinder Singh came by his bulldog, Watkins thought.

The judge instructed the clerk to call the next case.

The clerk told the marshal, "Call Singh!"

The marshal did, and another mass movement toward him followed. The marshal reminded the clerk that all the Sikhs were named Singh. She stumbled over a multiple-syllable first name, and the marshal didn't get it the first time, and while they were trying to figure out the right pronunciation, the judge called a ten-minute recess.

Watkins slipped out ahead of Pierre and Singh, and waited in the hallway for them.

Lawyer and client emerged soon afterward, Singh clutching *Exhibit-A*.

"See you got your bat back," Watkins said to Singh.

Singh held it up and smiled. "It's my favorite bat."

"Now he can really score some runs for us," Pierre said.

Singh stopped to speak to the other Sikhs in their language about their respective cases. Like him, they were gas station operators. Unlike him, they had been cited by the state Department of Environmental Protection for allegedly failing to upgrade their underground gas-storage tanks by a state-mandated deadline.

While they chatted, Watkins gave Pierre details of his meeting with Sarubbi.

"I'll just go ahead and sue the township for denying us a place to play," Pierre said.

"That's what I thought you'd say," Watkins said.

"What options do they give us?"

"Buying that piece of land would be our best bet."

"That's the long-term solution," Pierre noted.

"For now, let's do it Sarubbi's way."

"Sarubbi suggested we take our case to the Township Council; we did and the council is hanging us out to dry. Now he wants us to form an alliance with the soccer moms and start a petition. I say the time for schmoozing is over."

"Let's wait and see what sort of response we get from the announcement he's sending out about the creation of a youth cricket league," Watkins said. "If the soccer moms aren't interested, then we do it your way."

As usual, he had the last word.

******

After touching base with Gina during a break in her seminar, Watkins spent the rest of the day writing on his laptop at the local Starbucks. He got home shortly after 5 to find his wife at the kitchen table with a slew of documents spread out before her.

"How did it go?" he asked, refreshing her cup of fresh-brewed coffee.

Gina put down the booklet she was reading: *The State of Small Business Profile: United States*. "Did you know that there are about five-and-a-half million women-owned businesses in the United States?"

"Did you read the part that says most small businesses go under within the first three years?" he said.

"There you go again with your negativity," Gina said, slapping him on the hand with the booklet.

"Did you run your business idea by the workshop leader?" he asked, easing beside her, cup in hand.

"I sure did; now I've got to do the market research," she said, lifting another document from the pile: *Getting Started*.

"Well, I've also been thinking along those lines for you, and I came up with something that would be just right for you." He heard the tremor in his voice, and his hand shook as he brought the cup to his lips.

"What?"

"I'm not going to tell you until I've done the market research."

"Not even a hint?"

"Not even that."

Gina cocked her head the better to study him. "And when am I going to hear it?"

"Give me a couple days."

The phone rang.

"By the way, some man called a little while ago, asking for you," Gina said. "I told him you should be in shortly. That must be him."

"Did he give a name?"

"He said he was the Ambassador."

"Ambassador to where?"

"He didn't say."

Watkins lifted the receiver.

The call was for him.

The caller said he was Ellison Langston. The name did ring a bell: Langston had served briefly as U.S. ambassador to the United Kingdom in the Reagan administration.

"My granddaughter just brought home a note from the township recreation department about your plans to form a youth cricket league," Langston said.

The declaration jolted him. He turned his back on Gina and dropped his voice, "My number's not on that note, is it?"

"I got that from Mr. Sarubbi," Langston said.

Sarubbi should have known better than to give out his home number. Conscious of his wife's presence, Watkins thought of retreating to his basement office or telling Langston that he would call him back. He dismissed the thought; either action was sure to arouse suspicion. He merely would have to weigh his words.

"The information is correct," Watkins said, and started to panic at the thought that Gina might be overhearing Langston, though she gave no indication of this as she perused another document: *Writing A Business Plan.*

"My granddaughter is very sports oriented, and would love to play a new sport, so you can definitely sign her up," Langston said. "But that's not the real reason I'm calling. I thought maybe you might want to grace us with your presence."

The ambassador elaborated: He was expecting a very important visitor, a baron, whom he knew from his days as ambassador to the United Kingdom. The baron didn't golf. So, Langston was thinking it might make his British visitor feel right at home by putting on a little cricket game as part of a gala reception for him.

"When is the visit?"

"This Saturday," Langston replied. "I would have invited you earlier but this is the first I'm hearing about your cricket club. If you are free this evening, why don't you join me for dinner at the club. We can get to know each other and discuss your fee."

Fee? As in cash, to be used for a downpayment on the purchase of that prime real estate?

After the setbacks, the tide seemed to turning in the cricket club's favor.

Watkins was about to accept the invitation when a red flag went up. No way could he pull it off without Gina's knowledge. "Let me call you back."

He ran it by Gina after hanging up: "The ambassador is expecting a visit from royalty," he said, trying for a swagger in his voice. "He wants the cricket club to entertain his guest, to make him feel at home with a very British gentlemen's game on their nice lawn, with crumpets and high tea and all that jazz."

"And what member of the royal family is that? The queen?"

"It's a baron," he said.

"A baron is as far down the royalty chain as you can get."

"You and I know that," he said, with a forced chuckle. "But those WASPs on the Hill either don't, or don't care. It's the closest to royalty they're ever likely to get."

"Well, pass the invite along to the other cricket members. Let them handle it."

"The ambassador also invited me to join him for dinner this evening at the country club to talk about it."

Gina sighed, her shoulders sagged, and she had that look of despair in her eyes.

"Gina, the club is in crisis," he said, deciding to face the problem head on. "The middle school grounds have been taken away and given to Little League. The ambassador is willing to pay the club to entertain his guests. The club could use the fee toward purchase of its own grounds. What's wrong with that?"

"There's nothing wrong with it, but shouldn't he be talking to Patel? Vijay Patel is the new club manager, isn't he?"

"Patel's supposed to be."

"Then why can't Patel handle it?"

Because his wife showed up unexpectedly, and very dramatically, at the game last Sunday and discovered that he had lied to her when he said he was going to work, and now Patel is in the doghouse.

But dare he tell her that?

"Because I'm the one he invited to dinner," Watkins said. "It would be rather odd for me to call him back and suggest he invite Mr. Patel to dine with him instead."

Gina again sighed, more heavily, and looked away.

"If you don't want me to go, I won't go," he said.

"Fred, you're no longer involved with the club, so why is this so important to you?"

"Look, I founded this thing," he said, a little worked up. "It's important to me that it not go down the tubes."

"Nothing lasts forever, Fred."

"It's important to me," Watkins tried again, "because once in a while I'd like to go down to the grounds, with my son-in-law and grandson when they come to visit, to watch a game or two. It's much better to be a player than a fan, but I'm conceding that my one last game is over and I'd be satisfied being a fan. Is that being unreasonable?"

Gina got up abruptly and went to the kitchen counter, and began adding a coating of garlic salt to a chicken that was headed for the oven.

Watkins followed. He pressed himself against her, and hugged her about the waist. "It's not like I'd be playing, like I did last Sunday and risking a heart attack like Pops," he said, now gently rubbing his head against hers, kissing her ear. "I'll be organizing the game, that's all. It sounds like one of those dress-up affairs. Might even ask us to bring our wives."

"At the Fernwood Country Club? You gotta be kidding."

"You heard me speak to the man."

"Does the ambassador know you're black West Indian?" she said.

"What does race have to do with it?"

"Isn't that the place we tried to drive up to and the security guards turned us back?"

"That was a long time ago," he said.

"The same country club where the bluebloods meet, with their debutante balls and all that?"

"Coming out parties?" Watkins chuckled. "That went out of style. In any case, they cleaned up their act after Langston was nominated for the ambassadorship."

"I remember. Said at his hearing before the Senate Foreign Relations Committee that he didn't know there were no blacks or women or Jews in the club."

"As I said, they've cleaned up their act." At least, so he had heard. "It's a one-shot thing. Once it's over, that's it, I swear."

"Okay, Fred, you can organize your exhibition game," she said.

"Thanks."

He kissed the back of her neck, happily retreated to his basement office, called the ambassador back on his cell. "I can make it for dinner."

"Then see you at the club at 5."

******

His Volkswagen wagon refused to start and Gina had taken her BMW to the body shop for a tune-up. After finding out that a road service crew would take at least an hour, Watkins called a cab to take him to the Hill, as the elevated south side of Fernwood was generally called.

"Have you ever been up this way?" the cab driver asked as the taxi began its ascent up Magnolia Drive, the winding road leading to the Fernwood Country Club and golf course.

"Once, a long time ago," Watkins said.

"Well," the man said, "hope you don't take it the wrong way, but I've dropped off and picked up dozens of people at the club over the years, and I've never seen a black person there, other than the doorman."

"I suppose there always is a first time," Watkins said, but wondered whether Gina's instincts were correct, that the ambassador assumed he was white. *This ought to be interesting, possibly material for my novel.*

The driver let the passenger-side window down to give Watkins an unfiltered view of the kaleidoscope of European-influenced castles and mansions with their broad patios and balconies, domes, cupolas and turret, coach-houses and detached servants quarters.

"This is what you call old money," the driver said.

"Where's the new money?"

"That's the folks down in the gated communities with their security cameras," the driver said. "The folks below built their pretentious homes on their stock-market winnings. But up here, it's all inherited money. Railroad, oil, and gunpowder. The real power is right here in these golf course lots. Funny thing about it, most of the folks here don't golf. They live here because having a golf course address gives them prestige, real snob appeal."

The driver veered to make room for a middle-aged jogger who wore a baseball cap backward, then a woman walking a poodle.

"Most of these homes are occupied by one or two adults," the driver continued with his insights. "Their kids probably are off somewhere doing drugs. They show up to claim their inherence when their parents croak."

The driver, it turned out, was a bit of a local history buff. After Prohibition, he related, the Fernwood government voted to keep the town dry, but the liquor continued to flow freely at the club on the Hill among the township elite. Then, the story went, the police chief applied for club membership and was rejected because he wasn't a blueblood. The chief, who had turned a blind eye to the goings-on, retaliated by raiding the club and hauling off to jail the management and a number of high-power patrons on charges ranging from running a speakeasy to aiding and abetting in its operation. Word got quickly to the governor and the charges were dropped. The state legislature then enacted emergency legislation allowing the Fernwood Township Council to bypass the normal referendum process and to sell the Hill to a group of private investors who then were granted a liquor license to operate the club in the newly created borough of Manchester. With a population of less than sixty in about two dozens homes around the golf course, the borough generally still was considered part of Fernwood.

"See how Route 295 comes straight through Burlington County to Cherry Hill, veers around Fernwood, then straightens up again through Barrington?"

"Never thought of it, but it does," Watkins said.

"That isn't by accident," the driver said. "The folks on the Hill looked out one day and saw the highway coming their way. Someone picked up the phone, called the governor, and told him it appeared that the highway was coming smack through the Hill. Before the caller put down the phone, the highway made a detour around Fernwood, and the folks on the Hill went back to their cocktails and golfing. True story."

The driver continued to regale Watkins with stories while navigating the winding path to the white Colonial building with Roman pillars, a clock tower, and a rooftop garden and balcony.

"You might want me to wait for you," he said, after Watkins paid him the fare and a hefty tip. "I'll turn the meter off."

"Most likely I'll get a ride back," Watkins thought aloud. "If not, I'll call and ask for you."

With a salute and a "good luck," the driver drove off.

Watkins was immediately offended when the doorman, a rather large African American in a white V-neck tennis sweater, dark jacket and bow tie, refused to let him in. No, the doorman didn't think he was lying about his appointment with Ambassador Langston, but he wasn't about to put his job on the line if Watkins were. The doorman suggested — "No offense; I'm just doing my job" — that he wait for Langston in the lobby.

Watkins grew uneasy watching the dinner crowd arrive in chauffeur-driven Lincoln Town Cars, Rolls-Royces, limousines, and exotic cars. They were all white men who looked like stockbrokers. Then, emerging from a black stretch limo was a man who had to be Langston. He was an imposing, intimidating man with receding white hair and very bushy eyebrows, impeccably dressed in a charcoal gray suit and bow tie.

Watkins observed, a little awed, as the throng parted to make room for Ellison Langston. The words "Mr. Ambassador," "Mr. Ambassador," "Mr. Ambassador" echoed down the line. Langston acknowledged them with almost imperceptible nods, murmuring their first names, "Al," then "Bill," then "John," and "Harry."

Watkins waited at the entrance to the foyer. He moved forward to greet him, but Langston chose to focus ahead to the doorman. "Sammy," he murmured and Sammy smiled, gave a curt nod, and said, "Good evening, Mr. Ambassador."

Watkins stood, frozen for a second. Of course, Langston didn't know him. Still, he had been in reception lines. He had met the governor of New Jersey at an advertising-awards ceremony once. "And who are you?" the governor said then, grabbing and pumping his hands. "Oh, I'm just another advertising and PR person," he had replied, and she laughed at his self-effacing response and said, "Just another PR person! Of course, you're more than that!" He also met Jerry Brown, the former governor of California, when Brown was running for president, and Brown pulled his tie and said, "Nice tie." Then again, both the New Jersey governor and the former California governor were running for something and everyone within arm's reach was a potential vote. Mr. Langston wasn't running for anything. Not that he knew of, anyway.

"Mr. Langston?"

Langston looked around, scanned his subjects, eyebrows raised. He resumed walking.

"Mr. Langston?" Watkins said, more forcefully.

Langston stopped, again looked around. That voice again.

Watkins drew closer. "Mr. Langston?"

They were standing face to face, almost nose to nose. Watkins reckoned that Langston was a good half-foot taller, and had a clear view over his head, but surely, Langston must have seen his lips move.

Again, Langston turned to continue.

Watkins reached out to touch Langston on the shoulder. "Mr. Langston."

"Yessssss?" He saw him, Watkins thought. The man actually spoke, but it was more of a question than a greeting. Like the security guards that day he and Gina had driven up to the Hill, Langston seemed to be demanding, rather than asking, the nature of his business.

Watkins offered his hand. "Frederick Alfred Watkins."

Langston pulled back. "I beg your pardon!"

Had Watkins affronted him?

Watkins repeated his name, and Langston seemed puzzled. Perhaps he had forgotten about their appointment. A man like him would have a lot on his mind. He easily could have forgotten about their appointment.

"Cricket?" Watkins said. "Remember?"

There was a flicker of something in those deep blue eyes. "*You* are Frederick Watkins?" he said, with deepening puzzlement.

"That's me," Watkins said, with a cheerfulness he didn't feel.

Langston folded his arms. One hand came up to rest on his chin, striking a Jack Benny pose. He was thinking, thinking.

Langston suddenly thrust his face into his. "Are you sure?"

"That's what my wife called me when I left the house," Watkins said.

His attempt at humor didn't seem to work.

"You're the person I called about putting on a game for the baron?" Langston asked.

"We spoke on the telephone, yes."

Langston withdrew his face, and he was back in his Jack Benny mode, "Well, I'll be darned!"

Watkins felt the ambassador's stare. The man was totally confounded. Watkins stared back at the network of blood vessels that ringed the man's face. The cynic in him started to enjoy this, then he was empathizing with Langston, even wanting to bail him out by suggesting they go someplace else. Or, better still, perhaps Langston preferred to forget the whole thing.

Langston's arms dropped to his side. He inhaled noisily. "I suppose we might as well go in."

The minions were again paying Langston homage as he led the way down a wide hallway covered with a green carpet with embroidered ferns and lit by low-hanging chandeliers, past the lounge where old men with white manes and tortoise-shell glasses, white shirts with solid ties and Brooks Brothers suits were smoking fat cigars and reading the *New York Times* and *Wall Street Journal*, past the card and TV rooms where more old men with bald heads played cards, past the banquet hall where a Rotary Club meeting was underway, a local senator at the rostrum, and into a dining room.

The head waitress was waiting to escort them to a table that Watkins figured had been reserved for the ambassador so he could survey the hundred or so other white males and break the monotony by looking out the window onto the sixth hole.

"Where's the other gal?" Langston asked.

"Philippa?" the waitress said. "Today's her day off."

The waitress told them what the soup of the day was. The fish had a long, French-sounding name that Watkins didn't catch. He thought Langston must have lost his appetite because all he wanted were a diet Coke and a chicken something with another long, foreign name. Langston recommended the smoked salmon, if he liked seafood, but Watkins opted for the garden salad and said a glass of water would be fine. There was no price on the menu, and he reckoned that a plain old salad by any name couldn't be all that expensive - in case he had to pick up his own tab, even though Langston was the one who invited him.

"So, you are Frederick Watkins," Langston said.

Didn't he say that joke before?

Watkins saw no need to respond because Langston became preoccupied peering at his minions. He seemed uncomfortable, even nervous.

"Look at that!" Langston said, suddenly animated. "Just look at that!"

The sharp reference was to a young white man who had just entered the room, flanked by two women, one black, and the other white.

"You know," said Langston, leaning over to confide, "it didn't used to be this way."

Tell me more.

Langston caught himself, settled back. "So, you play cricket here in Fernwood?"

"For twenty-five years," Watkins said. This "getting to know you" meeting was turning out to be a Q&A. Soon, it would be his turn to ask the questions of Langston. And at some point they would get around to the purpose of the visit.

Applause sounded from the room where the Rotary Club was meeting. "Will somebody shut that damn door!" Langston erupted. A waitress rushed to shut the door and Langston returned his attention to his guest. "I always thought cricket was a British game."

"You thought I was a Limey?"

A hand, with lots of hair on the knuckles, reached out to pat his arm. "Please, I didn't mean to give that impression. It's just that I thought, being ambassador to the United Kingdom, I did see a game or two."

"It's also played in former British colonies," Watkins said. "In fact, more people of African and Asian descent play cricket than the English do."

"Will you excuse me, please?" Langston shot up and walked hurriedly through the room as if he had an urgent date with the urinal.

Watkins was amused. Then he became aware of the glances of the other diners and no longer felt entertained, but rather the object of their entertainment. How long was he supposed to endure this humiliation? Not a second longer, he decided.

He didn't leave a tip. All I had was half a glass of water, he thought. On the way out, he told the head waitress to cancel his order.

Watkins was hurrying down the hallway when he saw Langston ahead, speaking to the senator. He made a detour, went down steps with brass railings and was confronted with a closed door with a sign above it that said: *Private Facilities - Members Only.* He went in anyway and drew back at the sight of naked men ambling in and out spas and saunas, beneath showers, and on massage tables.

Watkins pushed through the mass of flab and came out of a door on the other side with a sign that said: *Members' Lounge.* A bow-tied barman mixed cocktails at a small bar in a corner and a white-shirted waiter took the drinks on a tray to more baldies at card tables and at black leather couches and La-Z-Boy recliners.

The waiter scurried toward him. "Are you a member?"

How polite!

Watkins pushed on to the EXIT sign, ran up another set of steps with brass railings that were being buffed by two old women.

Free at last!

Ahead was a shimmering expanse of green dotted with golfers in the fading light. To his immediate right was a green tent beneath which couples dined on shell-fish and red wine served by private waiters. To his left was a parking lot. He bolted for the lot.

******

Gina watched her husband devour the low-calorie dinner — the baked chicken, potatoes and string beans — and waited for him to cough up details of his rendezvous on the Hill.

He had walked more than two miles back, deliberately so, trying to calm himself.

"Aren't you going to tell me how it went?" she said, her patience exhausted.

Watkins gave her the whole story.

"Guess nobody told him you weren't blueblood," Gina said, not quite the *I told you so* lecture he expected, but close enough. "It's supposed to be nice this weekend. How about we ride down to Baltimore's Inner Harbor? We haven't been there for a while."

"I have a better idea," he said. "Why not call Maggie and tell her we are coming to Manhattan on Saturday? Kenneth and I will take the baby pram to Central Park. You and Maggie can go shopping."

He pretended not to see her startled reaction.

"What brought that on?"

"As you said, it's time I start being a family man again."

Gina really got carried away, suggesting they stay overnight in Manhattan, and perhaps get Maggie to hire a babysitter so they could all go out on the town - dinner, a Broadway play and a nightcap.

He was game. "It's been a while since we did something like that."

"And maybe," Gina prattled on, "go to Maggie's church in Harlem on Sunday morning, then have coffee and Danish at that little corner pastry shop where your uncle used to take us."

"Just like old times," he said.

Gina wrapped her arms around his neck, and rested her head on his. "Oh, Fred, welcome back. I do so love you."

But will you still love me when you hear my business idea for you?

CHAPTER 4

Thursday, May 3

After Gina returned from her power walk with her girlfriends, Watkins and his wife drove over the Walt Whitman Bridge to the Italian Market in South Philadelphia. They bought fresh fish ("Yes, leave the heads on," he told the vendor, contradicting his wife), fruit and vegetables.

Next stop was the Korean market in West Philadelphia, where they purchased breadfruit and other Caribbean staples. They bought beef patties and jerk chicken from a hole-in-the-wall Jamaican restaurant next door to the market and snacked on the spicy food on the way back to South Jersey.

The final stop was the Shop Rite. Watkins dutifully pushed the cart down the supermarket aisles while Gina cherry-picked sale items.

They got home around mid-afternoon. Gina wanted to go to the mall to shop for clothes for their outing in

Manhattan. She knew he grew restless trailing her from one apparel store after another and he was excused.

Gina had barely left the house when the phone rang.

"This is Ellison Langston," the ambassador announced. "I returned to our table at the country club after making a call and you were gone. Is everything okay? And are we still on for Saturday?"

Watkins mentally replayed the scene on the Hill and his first impression of Langston. As a former advertising and PR specialist, he knew the value of first impressions. Part of his ad-agency job had involved going to these dog-and-pony shows and being given only a couple of hours, at most, to convince a skeptical advertiser that you could devise a marketing strategy better than the other agencies that preceded you and the other presenters in the hall waiting to follow. Getting the job often depended little on the substance of your presentation or the way you acted or talked or dressed, and more on vibes.

Langston had given off bad vibes at the country club. Was he wrong about the man?

"I'll have to call you back," Watkins said.

Gina got home two hours later with a large shopping bag. He followed her into the bedroom. She spread out on the bed clothes she had bought for herself and their grandson. She then held each piece up for his inspection, while gushing about the deals she had gotten.

Watkins agreed they were nice but his voice and body language must have lacked conviction.

"Is something the matter, Fred?"

"It seems I misread the ambassador," he said, and told her of Langston's call.

A cloud darkened Gina's face. "If you're thinking of canceling our trip to Manhattan, we've made a commitment to Maggie."

"We could leave for Manhattan right after the game..."

She sat on the edge of the bed with those sagging shoulders that said so much.

"I told the ambassador I'd get back to him," he said, sitting beside her, rubbing her back. "Whatever you decide, I'll accept it."

"This game is important to you, isn't it?"

To say no would be lying and she would know it; to say yes would be to enter the unknown. "It's not *that* important."

Gina seemed to wilt further. She stared at the floor in silence. "Why don't you go ahead with the game? I'll drive to Manhattan on Saturday morning, and you can come after the game. I'll make an excuse for you. I'll tell Maggie the game was for a good cause. How's that?"

Bless her! "It's a good ninety-minute drive to Manhattan and I know you hate driving long distances on the highway," he said nonetheless.

"I'll take my time," she said.

Watkins held her chin up and kissed her on the mouth. "Thanks."

She forced a smile.

******

From his basement office, Watkins called the club members to let them know about the game.

Word of the event got around to businessman Raj Bhattacharya.

"That's where all the movers and shakers meet," Bhattacharya noted. "It would be a good chance for me to establish some connections."

Watkins had reservations about Bhattacharya's showing up to tout his plans to open a chain of Indian fast-food restaurants coast-to-coast and to finance the venture with a public stock offering, but no way could he say no to Big Daddy. He would just have to keep an eye on him, making sure Raj didn't make a nuisance of himself with the blue bloods.

Watkins called Langston to let him know they were on.

"That's splendid," Langston said with a put-on English accent. "It's a noon luncheon. We thought you and your teammates might want to be our luncheon guests, as well."

"I'll let the members know," Watkins said. "We will need to build a wicket for the game."

"Excuse my ignorance, but what's a wicket?"

Didn't the ambassador say he had watched a game or two in England? Watkins described a wicket for him: a sixty-foot long carpet in the middle of the grounds to serve as the playing surface for the batsmen (batters) and bowlers (pitchers).

Langston gave him the number for the grounds keeper for help in setting it up.

"Is that satisfactory?" Langston asked.

"Very satisfactory."

"Jolly good," Langston said. "I'll have the boy pick you and your teammates up in my limo."

Watkins lost it then. He was about to demand who the hell Langston was calling "boy" when he heard a click.

He had given Langston a chance to redeem himself and the man was screwing up again.

Pierre shared his sense of outrage, but not enough to back out.

"I suppose we don't have to like him," the club president and captain said. "It's a fund-raiser. What price did you quote him?"

He hadn't quoted Langston one, and explained why: "Have you ever dined at a fine restaurant where there was no price on the menu? It's understood that if you are asking the price, you can't afford it. Langston can afford to pay through the teeth."

"It would be like collecting punitive damages," Pierre said.

Watkins liked the analogy. He could always count on Pierre for that kind of lawyer talk.

"Even better, we could get him to pick up the tab for our land purchase and clubhouse," Pierre was saying.

"Anything's possible."

Pierre had an idea: Instead of playing among themselves, why not play against another team? "That way," he added, "it would be more competitive, and it would be good practice for us."

Watkins called around. All the league teams were booked.

"What about the Mad Dogs in Philly?" Pierre said. "I don't believe they belong to a league. See if they are available to play us a friendly."

He called Cunningham, the captain of the Mad Dogs Cricket Club. Sure enough, the Dogs limited their play to friendly games. But they were scheduled to be at the Merion Cricket Club on the tony Main Line the entire weekend for their annual tournament with other Mad Dogs from California to Canada.

"I don't suppose you want to play our B team?" Cunningham said. "Who's on it? Just a bunch of old, retired farts who can't make the A team."

"How old?" Watkins asked, and didn't catch his response. Cunningham was speaking at their clubhouse - the Dickens Inn in Philadelphia – and he and his teammates were stuffing their faces with bangers and mash, imbibing John Courage, Double Diamond and Boddington, shooting darts, and watching a videotaped cricket game on the telly. "How old?"

"Real old."

"How old is that?"

Cunningham inquired of his fellow Mad Dogs how old they figured the members of the B team to be. A big guessing game followed, and it grew heated. For a moment, Watkins thought a fight was breaking out.

"Littlejohn, they figure he's pushing sixty, sixty-five," Cunningham reported back. "Longfellow? Got to be at least seventy. Pennock...."

Cunningham went down the list and it got progressively worse.

"Broomhead's the captain," said Cunningham. "You've got to talk to Broomhead if you want to set it up."

"How old is Broomhead?"

"Seventy-eighty, it's hard to tell," he said.

"He still plays?"

"Bifocals and all," said Cunningham.

For lack of better competition, Mad Dogs, B Team, it was.

The shaky British voice on the phone confirmed that he was Trevor Broomhead.

Before Watkins could identify himself, there was a click on the line. "Who's this?" demanded a woman with a feisty, very American voice.

"It's for me, Miriam," Broomhead said.

"Is this another of your queer friends?" Miriam cackled.

"My wife's not well," Broomhead apologized.

"I understand," Watkins said.

"Weekend after weekend," Miriam said, in a growing rage, "year after year, an eighty-year-old man behaving like a kid at puberty…"

Eighty!

"Miriam, you keep this up and I'll have to put you away," Broomhead threatened.

"…Leaves his wife every weekend for sixty years to be with men!" Miriam fumed. "I should have known the day I met you that you were queer."

"Please, Miriam, be a good girl and get your fanny off the blower…"

Watkins listened uneasily as the two traded barbs. He thought of his own conflict with Gina over his love for the game and he shuddered at the thought that he and Gina might end up like the Broomheads.

Miriam eventually got off the phone. By then Watkins had second thoughts about asking the Mad Dogs' B Team captain for a game. The Broomheads' marriage seemed hanging on a thread. He didn't want to be the one to cause it to snap.

Watkins pushed the thought aside. "Understand your B-team doesn't belong to a league, that you prefer to play for fun."

"And you're looking for a friendly?"

"A friendly game," Watkins confirmed.

"It's rather short notice," Broomhead replied, "but I should be able to put a team together."

After hanging up, Watkins called Pierre with an update.

"Now all we've got to do is put together a strong eleven," Pierre said.

"That's your department," Watkins said. "Just make sure Napoleon Bonaparte isn't on the team."

"Come on, you know the guy was only blowing smoke."

"I don't care what Napoleon was smoking," Watkins said. "The fact is he violated one of our strictest disciplinary rules; no fighting or threats of violence on the grounds. Besides, Napoleon only plays for pay. We don't need to hire any mercenaries this weekend. We should have a full team."

"You're exaggerating the situation."

"Exaggerating or not, Napoleon's bad news. This game is much too important for us. We can't afford to have the hot-tempered Jamaican muddying the waters for us."

He intended that as the last word on the subject.

Watkins simmered down, then actually began feeling good about the whole thing. More than a chance to put some money into the club's kitty, this could be an opportunity to showcase Fernwood Cricket Club to potential corporate sponsors and to the parents they were trying to woo for the youth league.

He called Langston back. "As you know, we are trying to form a youth cricket league. We were thinking that we might be able to get parents to sign up if they saw the game."

"You want to invite them to the game?"

"As spectators," Watkins said. "They'd be separate from your guests."

Langston offered to have a tent set up for the soccer moms, and to arrange refreshments for them.

Next, Watkins telephoned Cindy Asquith. He told her about the game.

"Will Napoleon Bonaparte be there?" she asked.

"The general won't be there," he assured her.

"Shane will be happy to hear that," Cindy said.

"How would you like to be chair of our women's auxiliary?"

"Didn't know you had a women's auxiliary."

"You're it," he said, and she laughed hysterically. "I would have asked Gina, but she'll be out of town."

After telling her about the letter Sarubbi had sent out to parents detailing the club's plans to form a youth league, Watkins assigned Cindy the job of organizing a trip of the officials and coaches of the Fernwood Soccer Association to the game. He provided the number Sarubbi had given him for the head of the soccer association.

"Chances are they all have weekend soccer games," Cindy said.

"Tell them it will be in a beautiful setting. Tents on the greens, tea and cricket. Very English."

Cindy cracked up some more. "I'll get them out. And Shane definitely will be happy to hear that Napoleon Bonaparte won't be showing up."

"That's a solemn promise."

Watkins telephoned Erica Hobbs. He reminded the Philadelphia Inquirer reporter of the interest she had expressed in writing a story about cricket in Fernwood.

The game on the Hill would be a good opportunity for it, he said.

Hobbs agreed, but given the short notice, said she very much doubted she could make it.

He told her they would be playing for "royalty."

That got her excited. "I'll be there, you bet," Hobbs said.

"You might want to bring a photographer."

"You bet," said Hobbs.

CHAPTER 5

Friday, May 4

A fter organizing a brigade to prepare a wicket on the golf course, Watkins drove to the Sports Shoppe at the Echelon Mall.

During last weekend's game against the Jamaica Rebels, he had noticed that some of Fernwood's players wore sweaters that were a bit ragged. The game on the Hill would be their first gig before royalty and it was important they look smart and professional.

Watkins bought two dozen small, medium and large sweaters, then headed for the C.C. Morris Cricket Library at Haverford College in suburban Philadelphia. Part of the college's claim to fame was that it had fielded a cricket team for more than a hundred years at its home grounds, which was laid out by British groundskeepers.

The C.C. Morris Cricket Library, within the school's regular library, had its own claim to fame: It boasted the largest repository of cricket books, videos, and memorabilia in the western hemisphere. No one had ever challenged the assertion.

Watkins pored through the library's books and viewed snippets of cricket videotapes, seeking rules of etiquette when royalty meets commoners. Should they bow when introduced? Wait to be spoken to before speaking?

In his research, he found lots of images of royalty, from King George IV to Queen Elizabeth II, being introduced to cricket players at Lords, the most sacred of cricket stadiums in England, as well as of Prince Philip handing out championship trophies to team captains at the end of tournaments.

There was no mention of barons. Or any indication that royalty had a clue as to what the game was all about. Indeed, in one of the videotapes, the famous English broadcaster Jim Swanson asked King George, after the king had inspected a lineup, whether he was interested in cricket. The king replied no, but that he was interested in the well-being of his subjects.

Watkins was warmed by the response: the old goateed geezer sure knew the value of PR.

CHAPTER 6

Saturday, May 5

Watkins pulled into the parking lot at the Fox Run Apartments complex off the boulevard, where team members normally assembled for away games, got out and began counting heads. Twenty-five past and current players, plus Singh's bulldog, were spread out in small groups before him.

"Where's Cindy?" he asked Shane Asquith.

The Englishman reported that his wife was driving around in a rented school bus, picking up officials and coaches from the Fernwood Soccer Association. "She'll deliver them to you on the greens, as promised," Shane assured him.

A white Porsche rolled to a stop alongside Watkins' wagon, a blond woman at the wheel, a black man in white clothes beside her. The couple kissed briefly on the lips, and the man alighted.

"Heard about the game," Jamie "Pretty Boy" Cumberbatch said, swaggering up from the Porsche to Watkins. "Thought you could use my pace bowling."

Watkins tensed at the sight of the Trinidad native, who had struck him as being more interested in chasing a skirt than a cricket ball. "What happened to you last Sunday?"

"What do you mean what happened?" Pretty Boy answered, with seeming bewilderment.

"After the water break we discovered there were only ten players on the field," Watkins recalled. "Someone said they saw you drive off with a blond spectator in her Porsche."

"I sprained my left thumb when you and I collided while trying to take that catch," Pretty Boy said, displaying a taped left thumb. "My lady friend saw the swelling and offered to take me to the drugstore to get something to tape it up. I left a message I'd be right back. Didn't you get the message?"

"And I guess you got lost on the way back."

"Her car broke down," Pretty Boy said.

Normally he would have sought disciplinary action against his fellow Trinidadian for his vanishing act, but, like Napoleon, Pretty Boy was a last-minute recruit in Sunday's game. They had needed players then, but that wasn't the case today. He doubted that team captain Pierre would pick nonmember Pretty Boy ahead of dues-paying members and alumni.

Raj Bhattacharya arrived with his son, Surajit. The teenager wore perfectly fitting whites that must have been tailor-made for the occasion.

"I'll be up later," Bhattacharya said from behind the wheel of his everyday Rolls Royce. "Need to tie up some business dealings with Donald Trump in Atlantic City."

Ahmed Siddique also showed up, in shrunken whites.

"I'm still working on that business plan for you," the Pakistani said.

"If everything goes right, the ambassador may give us a flying start by buying that piece of land for us," he told the investment banker. "So, be on your best behavior. We definitely want to make a good impression."

Langston's block-long stretch limousine arrived, with a light-skinned African-American chauffeur.

Fitzroy Chong, aka the Black Chinaman, went to his car and returned cradling a huge watermelon and a knife as big as a machete.

"I don't believe this," Pierre said to Chong.

"Why?" the Black Chinaman challenged him. "You don't eat watermelon anymore?"

Other players got on Chong's case. The Black Chinaman fretted as he took the watermelon back to his vehicle.

The limo driver opened the doors. Watkins arranged the seating based on height and leg lengths.

As Singh was about to enter with the dog cradled in his arms, the chauffeur said, "Where do you think you're going with that?"

The Sikh insisted on bringing the dog with him.

Watkins suggested to Singh that he follow with the animal in his own pickup truck.

"*Behnchod!*" Singh said, and kept on talking to himself in a not-too-friendly way, as he took the dog to the pickup.

Watkins also suggested to his neighbor, Michael Hankowsky, and son Timmy that they follow the limousine in Hankowsky's TV-8 van. The cameraman, who claimed he had talked PBS into hiring him to make a documentary on cricket in America, didn't have a problem with that.

Watkins climbed into the middle section across from Surajit. The teenager was fiddling with a coffee dispenser on the cocktail cabinet.

A helicopter flew low overhead toward the Hill. The chauffeur pointed to the chopper as he eased the limo out of the lot, and said, "Looks like the governor."

Watkins tried to relax. A lot of frenetic planning had gone into the match — now dubbed *The Colonies vs. The Motherland* — and he so wanted it to go right. He had cautioned the players, collectively and individually, to be on their best behavior. No need to get emotional on the field, as they had in the game against Jamaica Rebels. Remember, it was an exhibition game. In front of royalty, to boot; a chance to showcase the sport before an audience with a deep pocket and the ability to set up Fernwood Cricket Club for life.

In the best-case scenario, so many good things would flow from today's game.

And the worst?

Watkins didn't want to think about it.

Studying the bright faces pressed against the windows and necks craned to take in the view, Watkins saw a great bunch of guys. Warm. Friendly. No, he was worrying needlessly.

The parking lots to the front and sides of the club-house were a sea of exotic cars and limos.

"You can buy me that Excalibur for my birthday," said Ramuth, operator of a chain of outpatient health clinics, to no one in particular.

"Wouldn't you prefer the Lamborghini?" asked Siddique.

Sammy, the doorman with his trademark sweater vest, bow tie and plastic smile, kept bobbing his head toward the oncoming crush of formally attired guests. Strains of violins: *Pomp and Circumstance.*

"They're playing our song," the Black Chinaman said.

The music came from a live orchestra on a bandstand at the side of the building. Chong began humming:

"Land of hope and glory
Mother of the free...."

The Black Chinaman waved an imaginary baton and hummed and half-sang snippets of lyrics to the classic tune, and Watkins was transported back, way back to the days of a well-scrubbed schoolboy in khaki pants and navy blue shirt, standing in line waving a little Union Jack at a white woman in a large hat seated in the back of a sleek car with the top down, her hand raised as a police band played songs rejoicing in the glory of the British empire and pledging allegiance to the motherland.

He snapped out of it to peer out at Langston's guests. They had spilled out from the clubhouse onto the adjoining rooftop garden of the greens keeper's building overlooking the course. Servers in white shirts and black trousers moved among them with trays of drinks and finger food.

The limo arrived at the top of the Hill, and Watkins looked out onto vast greenery with several man-made lakes and streams that reflected blue skies. They descended through a wooden gate with a sign that warned about alarms and the prosecution of trespassers.

The chauffeur navigated the limo along winding paths, up and down slopes, across bridges, past a small chapel where a wedding ceremony had just ended and the bride and groom and their party waited at a gazebo to be photographed and the photographer was shooing away golfers who were chipping and putting away in the background.

The driver stopped at the grounds maintenance building with a sign: *Slow, golf cart crossing.*

A woman dragging a golf cart crossed.

"Can anybody just show up and golf?" Pretty Boy asked the chauffeur.

"Why, are you thinking of taking up golf?"

"Maybe." Pretty Boy depressed the button that lowered his window and stuck his head out. The woman turned. He smiled. She smiled back. She was late twenties, pretty, in cap and white top and shorts.

"You've got to be a member, or be invited by a member," the chauffeur said.

"Coffee anyone?" said Surajit, the teenager, who finally had figured out how the thing worked.

"I'll take a cup," said Superville, the janitorial service operator. "Black, no sugar."

"Extra cream in mine," said Pretty Boy, waving bye-bye to the female golfer, who waved back.

A city of rainbow-colored tents and picnic umbrellas had sprouted around an English teahouse and garden. Two Venable's Catering vans were parked near the teahouse. Servers in white-and-black outfits toted covered trays from Venable's vans to the teahouse. Another crew placed white cloths on tables beneath the tents.

The limo cruised to a field just beyond the tent and umbrella city.

"There's the field," said Watkins, with pride.

Hours earlier, he and his brigade had met with the greens keeper and picked out a spot between two slopes. The greens keeper had gotten his crew to remove a strip of turf for the wicket. Pierre had delivered the club's sixty-six foot long carpet and the workers had tucked it into the excavated strip. Flags were put up to define the boundaries. Within the playing area were two sand traps, a creek and a tree, all obstacles likely to interfere with play but that, the greens keeper had said apologetically, was the best he could do.

"And I see The Mothers are here," said Siddique.

"More like The Grannies," Chong said.

Watkins couldn't agree more as he scrutinized the group of elderly men in white clothes in the middle inspecting the wicket. Two other men, one in a wheelchair, the other in a lawn chair, were beneath a shade tree beyond the flags.

The chauffeur stopped the limo alongside the two men beneath the shade tree.

"The Over-The-Hill-Gang versus The Geritol Brigade," Chong snickered. "This ought to be good."

"Watch it, guys," Watkins cautioned. He stepped out and the wheelchair advanced. Watkins put on a smile.

"Freddie Watkins, I presume?" said the wheelchair driver.

Watkins estimated his age at sixty, sixty-five. Because he hadn't described himself to the Mad Dogs on the phone, he assumed that the man recognized him from his distinctive manager's blazer. "Trevor Broomhead, I take it."

"Trevor Broomhead, captain of The Motherland," confirmed the frail, lanky man with the English accent. His fingers were all bones and gripped Watkins' hand like a vise. "Bloody nice day for cricket, I'd say."

Watkins agreed, looking up into the cloudless sky and sniffing the country-club air. It was in the mid-70s, and supposed to stay there for most of the day.

"Let me introduce you to the other members of our squad," said Broomhead.

Broomhead started with Coopersmith, who had dozed off in the lawn chair, his head resting on his left shoulder.

"Hey, Coop!" Broomhead barked. "The Colonies are here!"

Coop shot up like a jack-in-the-box. "A hundred before lunch!" he said, and began applauding. "Jolly good going! Jolly good!"

Broomhead confided in a lowered voice, "Coop's grandson plays for Warwickshire. Grandson recently wrote Coop to say he scored a century before lunch in his last outing."

"I see."

"Don't be too concerned," Broomhead said. "It only happens when he dozes off."

Coopersmith returned to reality, and Broomhead told him that Watkins was here.

Coopersmith cupped an ear. "What!"

"Watkins!" Broomhead barked, and turned to Watkins. "He doesn't hear too good."

But he must have had twenty-twenty vision for he saw Singh's dog charging their way and did a Michael Jackson backward shuffle. Once past them, the animal darted between the tree and the wheelchair and raced across the greens.

Singh ran after the dog. "*Arre saala kutta, kahan bhagta hai?*" he screamed. "*Ruk jaa, kambakht!*"

Watkins watched Singh close the gap and step on the leash. His foot was pulled from beneath him and he toppled to the turf. "*Ruk jaa, kambakht!*"

The dog went through tent city. Watkins heard a woman scream and the sound of falling trays within the tent. The animal reappeared beyond the enclave, Singh in pursuit. Both vanished over a hill.

Calm down or you'll blow a gasket, Watkins told himself. It was an accident. No real harm done.

Pierre said in his ear, "Whatever you do, don't tell them we'll pay for the damage."

Watkins introduced Pierre to Broomhead. In turn, the captain of Mad Dogs introduced them to the other members of his squad. Watkins observed that some of the opposition players were not only way past their prime, but also into their second childhood. Heygate, the vice captain, walked with the aid of a cane.

But they appeared to be a spirited bunch as they debated the amount of moisture in the air, the wind direction, the angle of the sun, and whether all these factors made it a bowler's or a batsman's wicket.

Watkins counted ten Mad Dogs, not including Broomhead.

"Do you play?" he asked Broomhead.

"Some blokes object to me in the outfield in my cricket-mobile, as I call my mobile chair," Broomhead replied. "But I've been told you chaps from The Colonies are good sports."

"We are."

"The recommended speed is ten an hour, but I have a customized unit that can go up to forty. That's miles per hour, not gallons." To prove the point, Broomhead sped off in the motorized gadget back to Coopersmith beneath the tree.

Watkins heard snickering at his back.

"Don't say a word," he cautioned his teammates.

A man in a business suit came down from tent city and let them know he was Mr. Venable, the caterer, and that he had a special tent — the one off to the side — set up for the players and their guests, if they had any. He had assigned two of his waitresses to the moms.

Watkins made the announcement to the players, and began handing out the sweaters he had bought for the occasion so his team could pose for pictures. Broomhead offered to take the pictures. He handed Broomhead his camera, and took his usual position, end of first row on the left.

Hankowsky set up his camera on a tripod, hit the self-timer button, and he and Timmy got into the video he claimed to be making for PBS.

Watkins, with an assist from Pierre, went over the ground rules with Broomhead: Because of the irregular shape of the field and the obstacles within it, many of the normal rules of play would have to be set aside. Any "natural" interference of the ball — such as its being stopped by the tree, stuck in the sand traps, or ending up in the creek - would be an automatic two runs. If the ball crossed the flags on the right side of wicket, a distance of fifty yards, that would be an automatic four runs. Past the flags on the left side, a much shorter distance of thirty yards, would be two runs.

Next, Watkins borrowed two sets of chairs and tables from the teahouse and placed them beneath the shade tree. He labeled one *Press* and the other *Scorers' Table*. Pierre had created a six-foot-high scoreboard, replete with lettering - *Colonies vs. Motherland*. He helped the captain set up the contraption.

Pierre sat at the scorers' table, scorebook in hand. Watkins didn't envy the captain's task: He had twenty-five players from whom to choose an eleven. That meant that fourteen guys who didn't make The Colonies lineup were going to be pissed off. Would they create a scene?

111

Aware of Pierre's dilemma, the players broke themselves up into three groups. One did pushups; another practiced catching; the third group worked on fielding.

Watkins took pictures.

"That should be a jolly catch," Broomhead commented from his chair as Sankar, the shrink, moved to catch a ball that had been batted sky high.

At the last second, the shrink pulled back and allowed the ball to fall in front of him. "Don't hit it so high," he protested.

Pierre struck Sankar off his list.

It didn't take long for others to disqualify themselves. The old timers, who had dragged themselves out of retirement in ill-fitting whites, were the first to go. Ramuth, the health-care chain operator, split his pants trying to take a sharp catch to his right. Smith, the butcher, twisted a foot in a sand trap and sprained the ankle while chasing a ball. Superville, the janitorial service operator, oblivious of the calls to "Watch it!" fell backward into the creek while backpedaling to take a catch. Siddique threw a wild pitch ("Sorry! Sorry! Sorry!" he cried as the ball left his hand) that struck the Black Chinaman's head when Chong turned and attempted to duck. Beresford, the barber, pointed to his arthritic shoulder to explain why he hand-carried instead of throwing back the ball to the bowlers.

Pierre struck their names and looked around for more candidates.

A caravan of golf carts came down the lane to the tea-house. About two hundred people stepped out.

"Looks like lunch is served," said Chong, massaging the back of his head. "I could use a drink."

A man in a dark, pinstriped suit came toward them.

"That has to be The Man," Pierre said, a little awed.

Ellison Langston had the air of a man of considerable wealth and influence, the quintessential country club blueblood.

"That's our man Langston," Watkins confirmed.

He greeted and introduced Langston to the Fernwood players. Broomhead did likewise with his teammates.

"The game will begin at 1, right after lunch," Langston told the two captains. "It will begin with an inspection of your troops by the baron and the governor. I believe that's how they do it at the start of professional ..."

Langston broke off. Bushy eyebrows arched upward, and he squinted. Watkins followed the ambassador's gaze and saw Singh chasing the bulldog across a hillock. The Sikh had lost his turban. With his hair blowing about, he looked like a spaced-out rocker on stage. Man and animal vanished on the other side of the hillock.

"What is it, Mr. Ambassador?" Pierre challenged Langston.

"I thought I saw...."

"Saw what?" Watkins joined the challenge.

"Never mind," Langston said, with a wave of the hand. "Come. Let's grab some lunch."

"About time," the Black Chinaman said beneath his breath.

They followed Langston to his personal tent, where one of the tables had a sign that read: *Team Officials*. Watkins sat at that table with Pierre, Broomhead and Coopersmith. There was room for two more at the table. The Black Chinaman and the shrink came over.

Servers appeared. They poured coffee and strong-brewed British tea and offered a choice of appetizers:

prawn cocktail with brown bread and butter, smoked salmon with horseradish *crème fraiche*, and melon with port wine and ground ginger.

"See?" Chong pointed to the half-cut melon on a dish before him. "Should have brought my own melon."

"Be careful what you say," Sankar, the shrink, whispered and pointed with a thumb at Coopersmith, whose head was resting on his own shoulder and who appeared to be eavesdropping.

"The man's deaf," Chong said.

Watkins made small talk with Broomhead as they tackled the prawns. Coopersmith sipped tea, and burped.

"Try not to gurk at my table, will you, old boy?" Broomhead rebuked Coopersmith.

The orchestra members moved down from the clubhouse and set up beneath a shade tree on the fringe of the encampment, and Chong again hummed along:

"*Rule Britannia*
Rule Britannia
Britannia rules the waves…"

Pierre kept trying to make conversation with Coopersmith next to him, but after finishing his appetizer, the Mad Dog appeared to have dozed off again.

Raj Bhattacharya, accompanied by a bodyguard in black, materialized among them. He wore a two-button, single-breasted navy sports coat, a Brooks Brothers button-down dress shirt with open collar, brown belt with a gold buckle that matched the buttons on the jacket, and, like Langston, British tan gabardine trousers. His hair had turned jet black and was slicked back. A pair of binoculars dangled like an oversized pendant from a shiny necklace.

Watkins started to rise. "I'll introduce you to the ambassador."

"Sit down." Bhattacharya had assumed the air of a host checking on his guests. "I'll find my way around."

Bhattacharya raised the binoculars to his eyes, and zoomed in on the governor and ambassador two rows over. The two high officials stood speaking to a man with a receding hairline. Two uniformed state troopers stood behind them. Bhattacharya put away the binoculars, donned a pair of dark glasses, and ambled over. The troopers moved to intercept him, but too late: Bhattacharya already was introducing himself.

Servers appeared pushing food-laden trays.

"Wonder what they're feeding us?" Chong wiped his lips with a table napkin after consuming the last prawn on a bed of lettuce with pink mayonnaise. "Being commoners, we probably will be fed boiled salt beef and carrots and dumplings with wow-wow sauce."

He couldn't have been more wrong. They had a choice of entrees: roast sirloin beef with Yorkshire pudding, beef Wellington, braised lamb shank with baby potatoes, prime rib of beef *au jus* with horseradish cream, smoked haddock or grilled Dover sole, chicken with bread sauce, shepherd's pie, and peas and faggots.

"Faggots!" Chong exclaimed.

"Yes, me luv," said the English-sounding waitress. "They're meatballs made out of innards - liver, kidneys, hearts - in gravy, with mushy peas. Would you like to try some?"

"I pass," said Chong. "I'll have the beef Wellington."

Watkins chose the smoked haddock.

Seated at an adjoining table, Siddique asked the server, "Is it halal meat?"

The server appeared stumped.

"You are really finicky about your brand of meat, aren't you?" Heygate, the Mad Dogs' vice captain seated next to him, said to Siddique.

Watkins did another head count. It seemed everyone was there except Pretty Boy and Singh. He couldn't recall seeing Pretty Boy during the warm-ups and wondered where he might be.

"What's for afters, Hon?" Broomhead asked the waitress as she cleared plates from their table.

For dessert, there was a choice of jam roly-poly, English sherry trifle, plum pudding, and spotted dick and custard. The "dick," the waitress explained in response to Chong's query, was a rich sponge cake with fruit, served with hot custard.

"It's quite delicious," Broomhead said.

Watkins sampled it. They awaited his verdict.

"She's right; it's quite tasty," he said.

His teammates also ordered "the dick," as did Coopersmith after being awakened.

"I see you still have a prime beef *au jus* on your tray," Broomhead said to the waitress. "I'll take it. I'll also have the plum pudding, and a cuppa, Hon."

"I'm afraid we're out of pudding, Luv," she said, placing the beef before him.

"What!" Broomhead said. "No more pudding!" He turned to Watkins. "See that Coop doesn't fall off his chair, will you, old chap?"

Before Watkins could reply, Broomhead was swerving his machine through the diners in the direction of Mr. Venable, presumably to register a complaint.

"He's quite a foodie, isn't he?" the waitress said.

Shane Asquith came over to let them know that the

soccer moms had arrived. Watkins looked to the other side of the encampment and saw a group of women and a young man with a shaved head. They stood in a tight knot in front of a yellow school bus. Unlike the women diners, who were all hats and laces, the soccer moms were casually dressed and wore dark glasses that reminded Watkins of viewers in old 3-D movies.

Watkins excused himself. He asked Hankowsky to escort the soccer moms to their special tent, went and got his cricket kit from beneath the shade tree, and ambled over. Three tables, covered with white tablecloths, had been set up beneath the tent for the moms. The tables were bare.

"Ta-da!" said Cindy, stepping out from among the guests, and waving her hands toward the moms. "They're all yours."

"Thanks, Cindy." Watkins smiled at the group. "Good morning, ladies, and young man. Welcome to the Hill."

No one replied, or nodded back. They looked in a foul mood. Cindy must have interrupted their Saturday morning soccer routine.

"Which one of you ladies, if I may ask, is president of the Fernwood Soccer Association?" Watkins inquired.

No reply.

"That's not a trick question," Watkins said.

"Come on, Frieda," Cindy said, staring at the woman in the front row, center, "'fess up."

She was a muscular woman with a heavily made up, scowling face. Watkins searched for her eyes behind the glasses but couldn't find them.

"I'm Frieda Kruger," the woman announced.

"Kruger?" Watkins felt and heard his heart go thump.

"Maximilian Kruger's wife," she said.

Watkins looked at Cindy for an explanation.

"What?" she said, grinning.

"Later," he said.

"And I'm Otto," said the lone male in the group, stepping alongside Mrs. Kruger.

Watkins recognized him then and groaned. "Don't tell me..."

"That's right," said Otto Kruger. "Didn't recognize me with my new haircut, did you?"

Watkins again looked at Cindy. Why would she inflict this on him?

Shane materialized and held wife Cindy by the arm. "I want you to meet some folks from the old country," he said, leading her away.

Watkins tried to convince himself that this was no conspiracy. There was no reason for Cindy to know that Max Kruger was the enemy. And because she didn't know, there was no reason to suspect that Kruger had sent his son and wife as surrogates to find out what he was up to, or worse, sabotage his efforts to create a favorable impression among the women as a first step toward creation of a youth cricket league.

Watkins studied his audience. Its members stood woodenly. Would his well-prepared speech work with this crowd?

"Cindy," he began, "has spoken to you about our game and our efforts to form a youth cricket league..."

"This," Otto Kruger interrupted, "doesn't have anything to do with your fight with my dad, does it?"

"Shut up, Otto," said a voice at the back. "Let the man talk."

Watkins deduced from the rebuke that his invitation had created dissension among the women. He needed to exploit the riff to his advantage. "Thank you," he said to the woman who was willing to hear him out. "What's your name, ma'am?"

"Vivian," she said. "Secretary of the Fernwood Soccer Association, and the first Mrs. Kruger."

The others tittered. All except Frieda and Otto Kruger.

If there were a chink in their armor, Vivian would be it, Watkins thought. "Do you have a teenage son?" he asked her.

"I sure do," she said.

"Anyone else?" He paused for a reply. "Oh, come on, cut me a break."

A sigh, and another hand went up in slow motion.

"There have to be more," Watkins said.

Two more.

"When last did any of you go out to see your teenage sons play summer baseball?" Watkins asked the foursome.

All hands came down.

"How come?" he asked.

No response.

Good, Watkins thought. "Let me try to help you," he said. "You don't show up at their games because the kids don't want you showing up. And the reason they don't want you showing up is because their friends might think they're a mamma's boy. No teenaged son wants to be thought of as a mamma's boy."

"Or maybe you don't go," said Hankowsky, who had joined them, "because your sons don't play baseball or softball, and the reason they don't play is because they don't appreciate the coaches yelling at them each time they strike out. They don't appreciate warming the bench."

Vivian said, "You're right about that."

"How many times," Hankowsky followed up, "have you been out to a Little League game and ended up consoling your kids because they didn't get a base hit, or hit a home run, or because they were made to sit on the bench? I know what it's like. My son Timmy took up basketball because he had such a rough time being a regular at baseball."

Watkins said, "We offer your children an opportunity to take up cricket, a gentlemen's game."

"What about the girls?" Vivian asked.

"It's a game for both sexes," Watkins said.

"Do you believe these morons?" Otto Kruger said. "Who are they trying to con?"

"Shut up, Otto," Vivian repeated. "Your daddy's no gentleman, and you behave more and more like your daddy."

The current Mrs. Kruger looked back at Vivian.

"We are here," Watkins said, "to introduce you to one of the world's most exciting games. It's a game without boundaries, involving people of all religious, racial, ethnic, social, economic and cultural backgrounds. All come together under one tent, as it were. That's the unifying force of cricket. If we all looked at life through the lens of cricket, it would be a much better world out there."

Otto Kruger began playing a make-believe violin.

"This," Hankowsky said, "is a cricket bat."

Watkins reached out to grab the bat, fearful of Hankowsky's intention toward Otto Kruger. But Hankowsky passed it to Frieda Kruger who passed it along without inspecting it.

"As you can see," Hankowsky said, "the surface of the bat is flat, making it easier to get base hits and home runs.

Plus, there's no such thing as a strike in cricket. You can go on batting forever. The kids will love it."

Hankowsky handed the current Mrs. Kruger a ball and she did the same thing, passing it along without looking at it. Watkins retrieved the bat as it completed its rounds. Hankowsky described the makeup of the ball and demonstrated the bowling action.

The two waitresses arrived, pushing carts with refreshments.

"It's time for tea," Watkins said.

Hankowsky said, "Tea and cricket are part of the tradition."

The women were mum.

"Perhaps you ladies prefer coffee?" Watkins said.

"Tea is fine," the second Mrs. Kruger decided and the others agreed.

The women took off their glasses, the better to study the silver teapots, then lined up with cups and saucers. The tea biscuits went fast and the refreshments seemed to relax them a bit. They pulled up chairs around the tables and sat. Even Otto Kruger seemed to have run out of gas.

Watkins reached for the packages of material in his kit. He had allowed Hankowsky to do most of the selling. It was time to close the deal.

"These are application forms that we would like you to distribute to your members," Watkins told the group. "Ideally, we'd like to have our youth cricket league formed by the time the park is opened on..."

Watkins heard a bang to his right and jumped. The women screamed and hit the ground as one. Watkins pulled back to allow two state troopers to run past. They had drawn their guns and were shouting for everyone to get down.

A puff of smoke appeared just beyond the top of the lane, then a beat-up Thunderbird convertible with the top down.

Watkins recognized the driver, and his heart began beating so hard he feared he was about to suffer a fatal cardiac arrest.

The Thunderbird backfired, puffed, sputtered, shuddered and died on the descent. The driver got out. He popped the hood and stepped back, fanning smoke from his face.

"It's just a car," one of the troopers called out.

The guests who had taken cover got up. They dusted off their clothes. Watkins heard wild chattering around him as to the identity of the intruder who had created the calamity.

Watkins fumed at the sight of the Jamaican fast bowler in his whites. "Carry on for me," he told Hankowsky.

He rushed over to Langston's tent. He stooped behind Pierre's chair. "Thought you weren't going to invite him."

"Calm down," said the team captain. "Napoleon helped win the game for us on Sunday. We want to maintain our winning streak."

"One win doesn't a streak make," he said. "Besides, this is a friendly. The result doesn't count."

"It counts for bragging rights," Pierre said. "We'd be the laughingstock of Philadelphia if we let these Mad Dogs beat us."

"Tell me you're not paying him." Watkins thought it was the least he could hope for.

"I'll pick up the tab for this one," Pierre said.

Napoleon appeared before them, pulling on the gold chain on his exposed chest. "Got your message," he said to Pierre. "The car's acting up on me again." He pulled up a chair and sat at the spot that Broomhead had vacated. He poured himself water, drank to the last drop, then began buttering Broomhead's bread.

Watkins waited for Napoleon to acknowledge him, but the lanky Jamaican kept stuffing his face.

"The foods are on your left; the drinks on your right," Watkins said.

Napoleon looked up for the first time. "Did you say something to me, Massa?" he said, derisively, slanting his eyes and curling his lips in a menacing way.

Watkins wasn't to be intimidated by the bigger, more muscular fellow West Indian. "Your salads, bread and butter are to your left; water and coffee to your right, the entree before you," he said.

"Anything else, Massa?"

"Yeah," Watkins said. "Don't talk with all that food in your mouth, stop making those funny noises, and take your elbows off the table."

"That's it, Massa?"

"And don't lick your butter knife."

Napoleon stared at the knife, then at him, as if telegraphing his thoughts. He jumped up and Watkins pushed his chair back to get away. Napoleon's thighs banged against the table, spilling the drinks. He whipped out a handkerchief and blew his nose forcefully into it.

Watkins was conscious of heads turning their way.

Napoleon stomped off.

Watkins slumped into his chair as the servers cleaned up the spill.

"What's the matter with you?" Chong said between gritted teeth. "Why do you keep provoking the man?"

"The man has no class. None whatsoever," Watkins said. He tried to simmer down. Pierre didn't seem to appreciate how much they had riding on this game. Why else would he do this?

Watkins' blood continued to boil as he watched Napoleon pick up a ball on the field and hurl it into the far distance. Napoleon kicked down the Press and Scorers' table, then sat beneath the tree, bringing both legs up, placing his hands over his knees, and resting his head onto his arms.

"Are you ashamed of your own people?" Chong said.

"No class," Watkins said.

"And you have class?" Chong said. "Tell me: If you're such a classy guy, why aren't you sitting at the VIP table?"

"That's enough," Pierre said.

Singh rejoined them. The Sikh's clothes were smudged with mud and grass, but his turban was back in place. He had given up the chase after losing sight of the bulldog. Singh eyed the extra plate before him.

"Go ahead," Pierre said. "Broomhead ordered it, but didn't touch it."

Watkins watched, vacantly, as Singh poked at the meat with a fork, as a child would a coiled-up snake in the wild, seeking to determine whether it was alive.

"Is this beef?" he asked.

"You don't eat beef?" Pierre asked him.

Singh wrapped the beef Wellington in a cloth napkin "For the dog," he said."Maybe he comes back."

Langston rang a bell and announced that the game would begin right after dessert. The team captains signaled to their players that it was time to take to the field. Entire sets of umbrellas and chairs followed. The would-be spectators settled down behind the flags.

Watkins returned to the soccer moms. Venable had sent over two more servers with trays of entrees. The soccer moms had become animated and actually appeared to be enjoying themselves. Otto Kruger remained standing outside the tent, and he and Hankowsky were speaking heatedly.

"How far can the kids go with this game?" Kruger asked Hankowsky.

"What do you mean?" Hankowsky said.

"Can they turn pro? Make money?"

Hankowsky wasn't sure. He deferred to Watkins.

"If they get good enough," Watkins said, "they can represent the United States in tryouts for the Cricket World Cup. That's a tournament bringing the top cricketing countries together. But they do so for the honor of representing their country, not for the money."

"Where are you from, Man?"

"Why?"

"You're Jamaican, aren't you?" Kruger said.

"I'm from Trinidad," Watkins said. "I'm a Trinidadian. Trini for short."

"Is that what they teach you back home, Mr. Trini? That money isn't important?"

"Money is important," Watkins said, "but it's like Kennedy said, ask not what your country can do for you, but what you can do for your country.... But we can pick this up later."

Erica Hobbs arrived with a photographer. Watkins scurried over and righted the PRESS table for the Philadelphia Inquirer reporter.

"Guess where you come from this weather is considered chilly," Hobbs said.

"If you're referring to the sweaters, the players wear them because they look nice," Watkins explained.

She wrote that down in a little notebook.

"But don't they sweat in those things?" Hobbs wanted to know.

"Just a little."

She wrote that down, too, and gave the Mad Dogs players a hard look as they warmed up. They had formed a circle and were practicing catching, not too successfully.

Hobbs said, "Thought this was a young man's game."

"Age is irrelevant."

"But you do have to run, don't you?"

"You can have a designated runner, if you're not up to it," Watkins said.

She wrote those things down, and asked more questions while her photographer went off shooting everything and everyone who moved, until it was time for the "inspection of the troops."

Pierre coaxed Napoleon, appealing to his vanity, into joining the Fernwood lineup. Watkins gave the pace bowler a wide berth, busying himself by sweeping the wicket of imaginary specks of dust.

Fernwood's lineup was twice as long as the Mad Dogs'.

Team members stood stiffly, hands behind their backs as the VIPs came their way, with Bhattacharya in deep conversation with the governor. Watkins couldn't help but wonder what the opportunistic businessman possibly could be saying to her.

The newspaper photographer snapped away while Hankowsky captured it all from the sideline with his TV camera.

The inspection began with the Mad Dogs, with Broomhead making the introductions of his team members.

Watkins overhead Stanworth, at the head of the line, tell the baron that he was a Cambridge blue.

"Oh, yes," the baron said, sounding immensely pleased.

Kite, the next in line, was "an old Yorkshireman," and the baron was dropping names of the "great" Yorkshiremen of the game: Boycott, Illingworth and Sutcliffe, and "fiery Freddie Trueman; quite a colorful character, Freddie was, wasn't he?"

Churchill was a distant relative of you-know-who. "We're making sure the flag flies across the pond," Churchill quipped, and the baron said, "How about that."

Botham had a cousin named Ian. "Oh, yes, Ian, the last of the great English captains after Hutton and Cowdrey," the baron said.

And Botham said, "Don't forget Frank Woolley."

The baron replied, "Oh, yes, the pride of Kent."

Vice-captain Pennock told the baron that he understood he was a Lancashireman who once played for the Staffordshire League, and the baron politely corrected him, saying Pennock must have been confusing him with that other baron, that he actually was a Gloucestershireman, home of "Wally Hammond."

And so it went, all very down homey, until it was Fernwood's turn, with Bhattacharya preempting him by making the introductions. It was just as well, Watkins thought. He still hadn't reconciled himself to Napoleon's presence.

At the head of the line, Watkins told the baron he was from Trinidad. The baron replied, "Oh, yes." He spoke with his head down, and seemed to be squinting, as though the sun was in his eyes, which it wasn't. His lips barely moved, and the words came out from the corner of his mouth.

Watkins waited for him to throw out some names, but the baron must have drawn a blank, for he moved on.

The governor followed. She turned to Bhattacharya. "Mr. Bhatta…"

"You can call me Raj," Bhattacharya said to the governor, stepping nimbly to her side. "Team members call me Big Daddy. Whatever your pleasure."

"Raj was telling me about your club," the governor said, extending a dainty, gloved hand, which Watkins shook. She flashed pearly white teeth for the cameras. "Said it's a game that places great emphasis on discipline. I was telling him maybe you should introduce it in our schools. That's one area where we can use some discipline."

Her words had a soothing effect on Watkins. "We are in the process of organizing a youth league. Our goal is to take the game into the schools. The soccer moms are here to help us."

"How nice." The governor leaned over to her trailing press secretary. "Take note of that," she said, then suggested to Watkins he give her secretary a call, that maybe there was money left in the state's discretionary-spending fund to fund a pilot cricket program.

Watkins promised to keep in touch, confident that the governor wasn't making another empty campaign promise.

"Napoleon Bonaparte," he heard Napoleon, midway in line, say, and he shuddered. "I'm Jamaican."

"Ahhh, Bob Marley country," the baron said. "How's he doing?"

"Marley?" Napoleon said. "He's been dead years now."

"Isn't that a shame," the baron said.

Langston nudged the baron along.

The inspection ended with no further damage.

Pierre asked him to umpire, but Watkins begged off. He preferred to concentrate on the larger mission: getting the reporter and the soccer moms hooked on the game. Pierre asked Asquith, who had taken himself out of the game, to do the honors, but the Englishman, too, begged off, saying in a joking way that the Colonies might accuse him of being a Benedict Arnold if they were unhappy with his decisions.

"I'll keep score, if you want," Asquith said.

Watkins surmised that the real reason Asquith declined to be selected on the team or to umpire was because he didn't want to be on the field with Napoleon.

Pierre studied the other players, looking for another candidate. He hadn't yet announced the lineup. Asking anyone else to umpire would be making it clear that he wasn't on the team, and the reaction might not be pleasant.

Watkins sought to solve the problem offering to umpire if Asquith kept score and explained the game to the reporter and the soccer moms at the same time. Asquith was agreeable, and Pierre was thankful.

A white blur appeared in the sky.

"Duck!" Chong cried.

Watkins held his head and ducked.

A golf ball came bouncing their way. It was followed by a golf cart. Pretty Boy was driving, a female golfer seated beside him. Chong picked up and handed Pretty Boy the ball.

"Thanks," Pretty Boy said. He eyed the blond reporter.

"Keep going," Erica Hobbs said to him.

Pretty Boy hopped back into the cart. Watkins watched him scoot off, his companion waving bye-bye.

Watkins returned with his teammates to the scorer's table and observed Pierre as he struck Pretty Boy off the lineup.

Pierre added a name to complete the lineup and handed the scorebook to Asquith.

"Hey, you forgot my name," Sankar said, alarmed

"Resting you for the big game," Pierre said.

The shrink threw his bat down. "Don't insult me by putting Timmy ahead of a veteran like me."

"It looks good," Pierre said.

"Why do you think you need a token white boy on the team?" the shrink said.

"Keep race out of this," Pierre said.

"What about Surajit?" Sankar asked. "Why is a fourteen-year-old in the team ahead of a veteran like me?"

"We need young blood."

Watkins saw the reporter looking their way.

"Mind keeping your voices down?" he said, lowering his.

"He dropped me!" Sankar said. "A veteran like me!"

"I'm selecting the team on the basis of ability, not seniority," Pierre said.

"What are you implying? That I have no ability?" Sankar said, louder yet. "If so, how come you never mentioned it?"

"Can't you work this out later?" Watkins said.

"He dropped me!" Sankar yelled. "Me! Top bat."

"Come on, it's only a game," Watkins pleaded with the shrink. "I don't expect this from you."

He became more concerned when he saw the advancing cricketmobile.

The crowd parted to make room for the machine.

"Strategizing, are you?" Broomhead said. "I'd say, you chaps from the colonies do take your cricket seriously. We'll toss whenever you're ready. Well, soldier on." He threw the contraption into reverse.

"How would you like to bat first?" Pierre called out to the Mad Dogs captain.

"That's real decent of you," said Broomhead, hitting the brakes. The cricketmobile skidded several feet backward on the low-creeping grass. "Must warn you: It's a batsman's paradise out there, and some of our chaps are in good form."

"Since it's a friendly, no need for the formality of a coin toss," Pierre said.

"Splendid," said Broomhead. "I'll tell my men to pad up. Ta, ta."

"Why did you put them Mad Dogs in first?" Chong demanded of Pierre, as Broomhead sped off.

"I'd rather be chasing their runs than have them chasing ours," the captain explained his strategy.

"Yeah, but you hear what the man said?" said Chong. "It's a batsman's wicket."

Pierre turned to Singh, curled up on the ground, chewing on a blade of grass. "What do you think?"

"Me?" said the Sikh in alarm. "Maybe I better keep out of this."

Wise man, Watkins thought.

"What do you think?"

Pierre had addressed the question to him. Watkins hesitated. He wasn't happy with the decision, either. While looks could be deceiving, from what he saw of The Mad Dogs they were unlikely to score many runs, batsman paradise or not, not with the ball in Napoleon's hand. And when time came for Fernwood to bat, Singh was likely to top The Dogs' score with a few swings of his willow, ending the game prematurely, providing little entertainment for Langston and his guests.

But dare he tell this to Pierre?

Before he could voice his thoughts, Napoleon threw a ten-dollar bill down on the table. "Bet anyone those Mad Dogs don't score ten runs!"

"Whose money are you betting?" Watkins said.

Napoleon gave him an evil look and snatched the bill up.

"I wish you would consult with the team before you make your decisions," Chong said to Pierre.

"Come on, let's go out," Pierre said to the selected players, and turned to Watkins."Wipe your face."

Watkins became aware then of the sweat dripping down his face onto his blazer.

"You mean I'm not on the team?" the shrink tried one more time.

"You're not on the team," Pierre said.

Sankar picked up and stuffed his bat into his kit. "I think it's time I formed my own team." He slung the bag over his shoulder and walked off.

"He'll be back," Pierre said. "They always come back."

Asquith came up to Watkins. "Do the Mad Dogs have their own scorer?"

"I'll find out," Watkins told the Englishman.

Watkins mopped his face en route to the Mad Dogs' camp. Several Mad Dogs were warming up by hitting make-believe balls with their bats. Others hovered over Broomhead, who was writing down his team's lineup in their scorebook. Coopersmith was back in his lawn chair off to the side and he appeared to be napping.

"Do you have a scorer?" Watkins asked Broomhead.

"Unfortunately, we don't. Do you chaps mind scoring for us?"

"Not a problem. I'll give your book to our scorer."

"That's real decent of you," Broomhead said. "First, let me write down our lineup. Coop! Where in the blazes is our star batsman?"

"I believe I heard him say he had to go to dicky diddle," Churchill said.

"This is no time to take a piss," Broomhead said. "Oh, there he is." Broomhead had wheeled to confront Coopersmith outside the circle of players. "Hey, Coop. Pad up!"

Coopersmith didn't respond.

Kite, the Yorkshire man, tapped him on the shoulder. Coop remained stiff in his chair, head to one side, right hand clutching a bright red ball in his lap. Kite stooped, tried to take the ball away. Coop held on tightly.

Kite felt for a pulse, and jumped back. "Oh, shite!"

His teammates converged on Coopersmith in alarm. Each felt for a pulse.

Watkins reached for his cell phone. "Should I call an ambulance?"

"Fancy him popping off like that," Broomhead said.

"It's the way he would have wanted to go," said Churchill. "On a nice day for cricket, in his whites, facing the bowler's end, the ball in his hand, the wind at his back, not a shadow on the field."

It was fitting that Coopersmith should pop off in exactly that position in relation to the wicket, for Coopersmith, Botham said, was a crafty bowler, a legitimate googly merchant in his time.

"Especially with the wind at his back," said Stanworth, the Cambridge blue.

"He wasn't a bad bat, either," chipped in Guppie, the lone Aussie on the team.

"He was a useful bat," Heygate, the Eaton man, concurred.

The Mad Dogs took their hats off and bowed their heads. Watkins did likewise. No one seemed in any hurry to get an ambulance. So sure were they of their non-medical finding that the Mad Dogs proceeded to pay tribute to the man with spontaneous, heartfelt eulogies, each recalling an aspect of Coopersmith's life, from the curly-haired lad at a suburban London boarding school where he learned the fundamentals - his batting techniques were classic textbook, his blade properly aligned with the left pad when playing forward; as a bowler, he had an uncanny ability to hide the ball until the last second before unleashing it - to his glory days at Glamorgan, where the English selectors were said to have eyed him for the national team.

They grew misty-eyed recalling how Coopersmith had given up that opportunity to follow his heart across the pond to marry an American student he had met on the platform at Paddington station in the Underground. But cricket remained his true love and he was out every Sunday, spring through fall, on the fields of Philadelphia, despite failing health and a neck injury that caused his head to sag permanently to one side.

"Well-played, Mate," said Heygate.

"A well-deserved rest," said Churchill.

Although he didn't know him, Watkins identified with Coopersmith. The man's life mirrored his own. They had shared a love for cricket from their youth and, as immigrants, had continued their involvement past their prime. He stood ready to cancel the game. It seemed the logical thing to do.

"I think Coop would have wanted us to continue," Broomhead replied to his suggestion of a cancellation.

Heads nodded feebly, faces solemn.

"He was a sporting chap," Kite said.

"Let's win this one for the Coop," Broomhead rallied his men.

"We shall triumph," said Kite.

Suddenly, it no longer was a game to entertain royalty, but a celebration of the life of a man who was the epitome of the game.

Langston must have seen the commotion. He came over from beneath the umbrella set up for him and his overseas visitor and the governor. Broomhead gave him the news of Coopersmith's passing.

Langston stooped and took a pulse. "Gentlemen," he said, rising, "I suppose you don't wish to carry on, do you?"

"It already has been decided," Broomhead said. "The game will go on."

"In that case," Langston said, rather tentatively, "can we quietly wheel him away? No need to make a fuss and upset the guests, is there?"

Watkins saw Fernwood players looking their way. He went over and broke the news. Comments flew - one Mad Dog down before a single ball bowled, reinforcing the point that Fernwood should have batted first.

Watkins returned to the Mad Dogs' camp, still seeking their batting lineup, but everyone seemed in a daze and he hated to intrude.

Langston used a cell phone to call 911. He asked to speak to the police chief. He reported the death to the chief and asked a special favor: Could the police, as well as the ambulance driver, wait in the parking lot at the clubhouse so as not to cause a commotion among the guests?

The ambassador dialed again, and asked to speak to Sammy.

"We are now one short," Broomhead said.

Watkins offered to loan the Mad Dogs a Fernwood player. He thought the shrink would be the perfect candidate, that he would relish the opportunity to get even with Pierre by playing for the enemy, but he saw that Sankar was halfway up the hill and out of reach.

Without waiting for a response from Broomhead, Langston volunteered to take old Coop's place.

"That's real sporting of you," Broomfield said, and his teammates said it was, and joined their captain in a little applause. "He was one of our opening batsmen, you know," Broomhead warned Langston.

"Does that mean I'm the lead-off batter?" Langston said, sounding not too sure he wanted to go through with this.

"One of two lead-off batters," Broomhead explained.

"It's not that difficult, is it?" Langston asked.

"Not at all, it's just like baseball," Broomhead said, and proceeded to give him an accelerated training course for the job at hand.

Langston had a new concern: "Am I appropriately attired?"

Broomhead stood back to take better stock of the ambassador. "I suppose it would be okay if you traded your jacket for a sweater. You aren't superstitious are you? All that stuff about bad luck wearing dead man's clothes."

"I'm not superstitious," Langston said, but looked as though he wished to reconsider when Broomhead suggested he "borrow" old Coop's sweater.

It took three Mad Dogs to relieve Cooper of his sweater before Sammy the doorman arrived to drive the body in the back seat of a wagon with dark-tinted windows.

Broomhead completed his team's lineup.

Watkins ambled over with the Mad Dogs' scorebook to the soccer moms behind the flags. The moms' assigned servers refreshed their tea as Asquith and Cindy gave pointers on the game to the moms and the reporter.

Watkins gave the scorebook to Asquith, and said to the moms, "I trust you ladies are enjoying yourselves."

Vivian was radiant. "Thank you, Mr. Watkins. This is real nice."

"You people are all right," said the current Mrs. Kruger. The scowl was gone and she now could pass for anybody's mother.

"More tea, me Luv'?" a waitress inquired.

Vivian held up her cup. "Yes, please, Hon."

"Just sit back and enjoy yourselves," Watkins told the women. He felt his confidence returning. Things might work out, after all. "Shane Asquith will explain the game once it starts. If he gets too technical, ask Cindy."

"Yeah, right," said Cindy, laughing.

"Shane was saying the game lasts a while," said Vivian.

"Cricket is a life of leisure," Watkins said. "Next time, remember to bring your knitting kits so you can knit during the water breaks."

Otto Kruger and Hankowsky stood behind the women. They were still going at it. Kruger accused Hankowsky of being brainwashed, and Hankowsky responded that Kruger had a closed mind.

"You better start filming if you want to make that PBS documentary," Watkins said to Hankowsky.

As Watkins approached the wicket, Napoleon shook his head at him. "Man, you sure know how to kiss ass."

Watkins stopped and appealed to Pierre with his eyes.

"Just let it go," Pierre said.

The fuse in his head exploded, igniting every nerve in his body. "That's it," he hissed to Pierre. "The Jamaican is all yours."

Watkins started to stomp off the field.

Pierre ran up and placed his arm around Watkins' shoulders. "You walk off and the whole thing collapses. After you worked so hard to put this thing together, is that what you want?"

Watkins looked out at the dignitaries and the soccer moms and tried to suppresss his anger. "Please, after today, I want no part of that man."

"After today, we won't need Napoleon. Now, relax. This is supposed to be a fun outing. Let's have fun."

The cajoling calmed his nerves and Watkins took up his umpiring duties.

Pierre handed the ball to Napoleon.

Watkins was concerned by Pierre's decision. He waited until Napoleon's back was turned to voice that concern to Pierre: "Why are you opening the bowling with Napoleon? He might hurt somebody."

"Let's see how the batsmen shape up," Pierre said.

"Why not put on a non-bowler and toss them up some baby balls?" Watkins suggested. "Give the ambassador a chance to make some runs."

Pierre smiled to himself.

A distraught-looking woman in a jogging suit who obviously wasn't an invited guest wandered onto the field.

"Has anyone seen a poodle?" she asked of everyone.

"We haven't," Watkins said. "We're about to begin our game, lady. You'll have to go back."

The woman continued across the field to the tree line. "Frisky, Frisky, Frisky," she called into the bushes.

Mad Dogs' opening batsmen, Kite and Langston, strode out in matching red helmets, to a ripple of applause.

Langston was Batsman No. 1, to face Napoleon's first delivery.

Pierre allowed Napoleon to set his own attacking field. The Jamaican walked way back, almost to the flags on the perimeter of the field. As Napoleon was about to begin his run-up, Watkins saw the tiny Union Jack on Langston's bat and realized that the ambassador was holding his willow backward.

"Hold it," he shouted to Napoleon. He pointed out the problem to Pierre, who scampered down the wicket and assisted Langston in holding the bat the proper way.

"Okay," Langston said to Napoleon with bravado, "bring it on, baby."

Watkins signaled Napoleon to begin his run-up to the bowler's mark.

Napoleon's first delivery, hammered into the ground a few feet from the bat, kicked up and almost decapitated the ambassador.

Chong, substituting as wicketkeeper for the missing Vijay Patel, collected behind the sticks.

Langston, who hadn't offered a stroke, wanted to know what happened.

"No need to bowl that fast," Watkins said to Napoleon, after the ball was returned to him.

Napoleon gestured to him with a middle finger.

Here we go again, Watkins thought, and felt his blood beginning to boil anew.

He went over to Pierre fielding in the covers, and expressed concern for the ambassador's safety. A blow to Langston's head would spell disaster for Fernwood.

Pierre shrugged, still wanting to see how the batsmen "shape up."

Over on the sidelines, Bhattacharya had seized the moment. He had slipped into the vacated ambassador's chair. The governor sat to his right, the baron to his left. His bodyguard stood behind him with folded arms. Now, Bhattacharya was sharing his binoculars with the governor.

Langston started to swing at another hard Napoleon delivery. The ball flew past him before he could complete the swing.

This time, Pierre heeded Watkins' advice. "Not so fast," he told Napoleon.

"Let the Mad Dog bat," Napoleon said.

The third ball was another bouncer, only it didn't rise as high or swing away as much from the batsman. Watkins heard a loud, cracking sound and saw Langston fall backward onto the sticks.

A loud, continuous, mournful cry went up from beneath the umbrellas. Someone shouted for ice.

Watkins was running to assist the ambassador when he heard a piercing scream. He spun and saw that the distraught-looking woman had found Frisky — in a compromising position with Singh's bulldog near a clump of bushes. The woman was wringing her hands and jumping up and down.

Singh ran toward the animals. "*Arre jaanver,* get off that dog!" he screamed.

Watkins looked on helplessly and with growing anxiety as two state troopers ran toward the distressed woman, screaming at the bulldog to get off the poodle. When the bulldog didn't, but continued to pant with his tongue hanging out, one of the officers picked up an errant golf ball and hurled it past the running Singh.

The ball hit the bulldog on the left rump, and the animal jumped, with a yell. The dogs became unstuck. As the officers closed in, the bulldog darted across the greens, away from the crowd. The dog leaped over a ravine, then around a golf cart, and ducked through another clump of bushes.

A black man and a white woman ran out of the bushes. They were naked.

Watkins' head spun and he almost lost his equilibrium.

******

Watkins arrived home to find Gina's car in the driveway and his wife on her knees planting vegetables in her kitchen garden.

"Why are you still here?"

Gina glanced up and continued working. "What time is it?"

"Quarter to three," he said.

"You're home early, aren't you?"

"Is something the matter?" he asked, observing that she looked more distressed than he imagined he did.

Gina straightened her back. "I called Maggie right after you left to let her know I'm on my way to Manhattan and you'd be coming later. She was very upset. I tried to explain that it was your last official duty for the club. She didn't want to hear. She called you every name in the book, and others that you won't find in any Webster's dictionary. Such language!"

"So you canceled?"

"She would have ruined the entire evening getting on your case."

"She has every reason to be angry," Watkins said. "And you should never have let me out the house. It was a mistake going to that game."

He strode back into the house, and was foraging through the kitchen cabinet when she came in.

She stood back and watched him until she lost her patience. "Before you break down the shelves, can you tell me what are you looking for?"

"Where's the Excedrin?"

She found the bottle of maximum-strength aspirin on the second shelf, staring him in the face and unscrewed the cap. "How many?"

"The whole bottle."

She let him have two, along with a cup of water, and watched him swallow both pills in one gulp. Watkins expected instant relief, and when it didn't come he staggered up to the hot tub and crawled in fully clothed.

142

"Aren't you going to tell me what happened?" She looked down on him.

Gina listened to his long tale with a look more of pity than sympathy.

"So what happened to the ambassador?"

"They eventually revived him with smelling salts," he recounted. "He couldn't remember what happened."

"And Pretty Boy?" she asked.

"He's missing in action."

"Was he the one in the bushes with the female golfer?"

"Hard to tell. Their backs were to us. She, too, is MIA."

"And how did the baron and the governor react to all this?"

"The entire party broke up in disarray. The baron left in a limo, the governor flew off in her helicopter, and the soccer moms drove off in their school bus."

She knelt on the floor behind him. Watkins felt her hands on his shoulders, then the pressure of her thumbs.

She said, "Pops is in a coma after collapsing in the game last week; a Mad Dog is now dead; the ambassador has suffered a memory loss; and you are about to have a nervous breakdown. Don't you think there's a lesson somewhere in there for you, Fred?"

"I've learned my lesson. My teammates — former teammates — will have to find a way to get a playing field without me."

Gina pulled her back erect. "I so want to believe you, Fred."

"Believe me, Gina. Either I quit now or end up with a bleeding ulcer. Not to mention losing the people who really care about me and who I care about the most."

"You could start tomorrow by coming out to church, and joining the men's choir, as you said you would."

"And be baptized," he said.

"Oh, Fred," she said, in a swooning voice, throwing her arms around his neck. "I prayed for this day. The Lord has answered my prayers."

She resumed massaging his neck muscles, and began humming:

"I believe for every drop of rain that falls
A flower grows;
I believe that somewhere in the darkest night
A candle glows.
I believe for every one who goes astray
Someone will come to show the way
Oh, I believe. I believe..."

CHAPTER 7

Sunday, May 6

After dressing for church ahead of Gina, Watkins sat at his computer and typed a letter to Emile Pierre, President, Fernwood Cricket Club:

Dear Emile,

I hereby formally tender my resignation from the Fernwood Cricket Club, effective immediately.

Sincerely,

Frederick A. Watkins

Manager

The letter may not have been necessary. After all, he already had retired. But he had communicated his retirement orally last season, and Patel had been elected his replacement orally. There had been nothing in writing. This letter made it official. He was done, forever.

Watkins hit the "send" button in the e-mail box, received confirmation that the letter had been sent, and sat back, feeling relieved. After church, he would make the break complete by taking down the cricket memorabilia and pictures on his wall and putting them in storage. Or, who knows, maybe he might donate them to the cricket library at Haverford College, along with his blazer and hat. Maybe the library might assemble it in a special display case: The Watkins collection.

Mentally, Watkins calculated the hours he had spent devoted to cricket in America and he figured it came up to years. What a waste. Had he spent that much time on his aspiring career as a novelist he surely would have produced a bestseller by now. But you cannot roll the clock back. You press forward, learning from the past. Henceforth, he would work full-time on his novel. For relaxation, he would take up golf. The nearby driving range had a special on: Five dollars for a bucket of a hundred balls, and someone to help you with your swing.

Gina's perfume preceded her. "Are you ready?"

******

First, there was the regular service, about thirty old folks raising their voices off-key in praise of the Lord. Then, the meeting of the men's choir, at least the embryo of the men's choir — six guys, including Watkins, discussing plans to give a concert and to meet mid-week in the church basement for rehearsals.

The service lasted from 11 until noon. The men's meeting went for another hour. By then, word of Watkins' decision to be baptized had spread throughout the congregation and everyone wanted to congratulate him.

Gina stuck around in the special Bible class to wait for him.

"How did it go?" They were on their way home and there was a lift in her voice.

"Great," he said.

Truth be told, he thought it would never end. Fernwood was scheduled to play a home game today against Pakistan Cricket Club but, with the loss of the grounds, Pakistan had agreed to host the game at its home field in Newark. First game he would be missing in twenty-five years. He kept wondering through the singing and the sermon whether Fernwood had a full team, who was on the team, whether Pierre won the toss...

They arrived home to find a car that wasn't theirs in the driveway and an Indian man in a business suit sitting on the steps. The man rose to greet them. He clutched a briefcase and his smile was all teeth.

"Ahmed Siddique!" said Siddique to Gina. "One of your husband's old cricket buddies."

"Hi," Gina said. She rolled her eyes at Watkins and went into the house.

"Worked up the numbers...."

Watkins put a finger to his lip. "Shrrrrr!" He waited until Gina had closed the door behind her. "I intended to call you in the morning: I'm not involved in the club anymore."

"Since when?"

"You were there yesterday at the country club. You witnessed the fiasco."

"Oh, that." Siddique waved it off.

"Yeah, that! We expected to get paid. We expected to showcase the club to the soccer moms and potential sponsors.

But Napoleon had to ruin the whole thing by knocking down the ambassador with a fastball. That picture is likely to end up in the newspaper."

"I'll keep it short."

Siddique's assurance sounded familiar. That was what the window salesman had said and they almost came to blows after the salesman gave him this elaborate demonstration of the inner workings of the windows and he replied that he would think about it and the salesman insisted he sign right away to take advantage of the special they were offering. Same thing with the man who came trying to sell him baby furniture after Maggie's birth. He made the mistake of calling an 800 number he saw on TV, and before he could put the phone down, this character showed up on the doorstep wanting him to sign up for the entire line, furniture for each phase of Maggie's life, from cradle to grave.

Then there was the aluminum siding salesman...

The last person he wanted to get into an argument with today was a self-described cricket buddy.

"Perhaps I can come back," Siddique said.

He was playing the old reverse psychology game, Watkins thought. He saw a curtain upstairs move and sensed Gina's presence at the window. Watkins decided to be nice, at least hear him out. "Come on in, but keep your word and make it short."

The Pakistani kept craning his ostrich-like neck on the way to Watkins' basement office, telling him, as the other salesmen had done, what an elegant house he had and hinting that he probably had a lot of equity built up in it.

"You said you had worked up some numbers for me," Watkins said, not bothering to offer Siddique a seat and also remaining on his feet, hoping the investment banker would take the broad hint and be brief.

"I assume you want a setup where the members share equally in the risks and rewards," Siddique said. "The good thing about limited partnerships is that you have little bureaucratic tape to deal with. Is that how you would want to go?"

"That's what I had in mind."

"Factoring the cost of land, construction, cost overruns, and working capital, I'd say you're looking at a total expenditure of two-hundred-and-sixty grand," Siddique said. "These are all ballpark numbers until you get an architect to design the facility for you.

"You should try to put up at least ten grand of your own. That tells the banks you are willing to share in the risks. The banks would like to see a history of savings. But since, as a start-up, the Fernwood Cricket Company... Is that what you're going to call it?"

"That's a good working name, for now," Watkins said.

"As I was saying, as a start-up company you won't have a credit history. The credit-worthiness of the principals should suffice. I assume you're all credit worthy."

"I can only speak for myself," Watkins said, "but can we get to the bottom line?"

Siddique rested his briefcase on the desktop, depressed the latches, and produced an application for a bank loan. "The total package, as we discussed, is two-hundred-and-sixty grand," he said, passing Watkins the document. "You put up ten, borrow a quarter-million, at prime, plus one, sixty-month term. First payment $5,158."

Watkins glanced at the document and put it aside.

Siddique produced the business plan. He read off numbers from the cash-flow projections and passed the report along.

Watkins flipped to the last page of the three-page document and saw that Fernwood Cricket Company would lose five grand the first year, break even the second, and begin making enough money the third year to start paying dividends higher than what he was getting on the bond side of his own diversified portfolio.

They were the kind of numbers that he had hoped the plan would show. They would make the idea much more salable to members. But they did nothing for him now.

"I got a friend of mine to build you a website," Siddique continued. *"Fernwoodcricketcompany.com,* with an e-mail address. You can call it up right now. Pretty site, with links to dozens of cricket sites."

Siddique handed him a DVD.

Watkins accepted it mechanically.

"Everything I've got you is on the DVD," Siddique said, "in case you want to give a presentation to members or make copies for them."

Watkins tossed the disk onto the pile.

Next, the prospectus for *Bhattacharya Enterprises.* Watkins read it, to be polite. It showed the planned chain of Indian fast-food restaurants to be a sure thing.

"I was over at Raj's and told him I would be dropping in on you," Siddique said. "He asked me to give you this and for you to give him a call."

Watkins wondered why, if it was such a sure thing, Siddique was here to push stock like a stockbroker instead of beating off wealthy investors from his door.

"Sorry about being so short with you, but I'm not in a good mood," he said as he escorted Siddique out.

"I understand why you'd be upset," Siddique said. "Don't forget to give Big Daddy a call."

He made the call after seeing Siddique out.

"Know what?" Raj said after hearing Watkins pass on the offer to buy into Bhattacharya Enterprises. "Today's my sixty-second birthday. Couple guys you know are here at the motel having a drink with me. Why don't you come on over?"

"I'll try to make it."

Watkins stretched out on the couch. He needed his body temperature to come down before making plans for the rest of the day. Gina brought him a bowl of vegetable soup.

Gina was so convinced that he finally had turned his back on his old ways forever, especially after he showed her his e-mail to Pierre, that when he mentioned Bhattacharya's invitation for a drink she insisted that he go over.

"Bring me back a piece of cake," she said.

******

Surajit Bhattacharya was up on a ladder rearranging the neon lights on the marquee of the Sunrise Motel. Watkins noticed that two new features had been added: water beds, mirrored ceilings.

Big Daddy was cleaning out the pool. He stood next to a sign on the fence around it: *Please don't pee in the pool.*

"Some guests, they think the pool is for peeing," Bhattacharya grumbled as he poured chemicals into the water. "The urine content can get so high you can smell the darn thing."

Bhattacharya continued griping about the aggravation he had to put up with, about the welfare mothers who were dumped on him by the system and how they shoved their babies' diapers under the bed, and flushed them down the toilet, choking the sewer lines and causing backups; about the fights in the parking lot among unruly guests; about longtime, trusted regulars who sneaked out in the middle of the night owing him big money; about the drug dealers and other shady characters who set up meetings in his motel and the gunfights that erupted among them; about the young Chinese girl — "pretty little thing" — who could find no other place to slit her wrists than on one of his freshly made beds; and about the time they found the body of a Philadelphia mobster under the bed. He had been shot twice in the back of the head. Execution-style, the papers called it.

"Tell you, Watkins, you just don't know the aggravation of running a motel." Bhattacharya stepped around the edge of the pool as he poured. "People think it's easy, that all you do is open the door and wait for guests to come in."

Father and son were dressed in dirty work clothes, and Watkins thought that, for a man who was supposed to be celebrating a birthday, Bhattacharya sure was working hard and sounding really grouchy.

Watkins empathized with the businessman. No wonder he wanted to branch out into the restaurant business.

"Am I too early for the party?"

"Why don't you go on upstairs," Raj said. "I'll join you."

Raj's daughter let him in behind the counter. Watkins climbed the steps to the second floor. He got to the top and was stunned.

Pierre was seated behind Bhattacharya's desk. Chong and Napoleon were seated on the couch.

"Why don't you come on in so we can thrash out this matter," Pierre said.

Watkins turned to leave. The Black Chinaman anticipated him, and shut the door. "You're not going anywhere."

"We canceled our game today," Pierre said.

"Why?" He didn't care, Watkins told himself. Just curious.

"I got your e-mail," Pierre said. "I showed it to the guys. It was a downer. We canceled the game so we could get things straightened out."

"You're wasting your time," Watkins said.

"I understand the way you feel about Napoleon," Pierre said. "But if you have to blame anybody for what happened yesterday, blame me. I'm the captain. You told me not to put him on to bowl. I should have listened. It's just that I wanted to win very badly against those Mad Dogs."

"I'm a serious cricketer," Napoleon said. "I play to win, okay? You stand in front of me with a bat in your hand, I don't care whether you're a teenager or an old man, I lick you down."

"Hear that?" Watkins shook his head in despair. "That's the kind of ignorance I'm talking about."

"You're from Trinidad, right?" Napoleon was on his feet, advancing, backing Watkins against the wall. "You've got something against Jamaicans?"

"Pops, my best friend, is Jamaican," Watkins said.

"Pops is at death's door," Napoleon said, ignoring

Chong's restraining hand on his chest. "So, what you're saying is that the only good Jamaican is a dead Jamaican?"

Watkins again turned to Pierre. "I told you: The man has no class whatsoever."

"What are you saying?" Napoleon snapped at him. "That only ass kissers have class?"

Something inside him snapped, and Watkins swung a clenched left fist. It landed on Napoleon's chin. The Jamaican didn't go down. Instead, he put up clenched fists.

Watkins felt Pierre's arms clamp around him from behind. Chong put a similar hold on Napoleon.

"I want a piece of that Trini!" Napoleon snarled. "Let me have him!"

Pierre hustled Watkins out of the room and into a small, adjoining bedroom, and shoved him down onto the narrow bed. "Don't move!"

As he cooled down, Watkins became conscious of the blood on his right knuckles. He probed for broken bones.

On the other side of the wall, the kicking and the snarling eventually subsided.

Pierre was back. "You're okay?"

"I'm okay."

He allowed Pierre to lead him back to the office. Framed portraits of Bhattacharya family members and papers were on the floor. Chong was cleaning up. Napoleon was back on the couch. Watkins expected to see a gash beneath his chin. Or at least a fist impression. Not even that.

Pierre faced Watkins. "You hit the man. Totally unprovoked. He can sue you for your lump sum retirement package, and he'd probably win, too. But he's not going to do that. An apology will suffice."

Sanity had returned. Watkins apologized and offered

his hand. Napoleon looked at it, with his characteristic snarl.

"Shake the man's hand," Pierre ordered.

Disdainfully, Napoleon shook.

"Sit," Pierre said, pulling up a chair for Watkins.

He sat.

Pierre said, "First thing we've got to agree on right here and now is that we have to end whatever feelings of insularity exist among us. You're from Trinidad, I'm from Antigua, Chong's from Barbados, and Napoleon here is Jamaican. But you know what? We are in America now and as far as Americans are concerned we are all Jamaicans."

"Or Haitians," said Chong. "Or Africans."

Pierre said, "And this class business you keep throwing in people's face; that has to stop."

"You aren't back home," the Black Chinaman said. "The only class in this country is green, the color of money. Green like the country-club grass we played on yesterday. Either you got it or you don't."

Pierre said, "If we can't get along with ourselves, how do we expect to fight the powers that be and get back our little patch of green?"

Watkins said, "Some of us build bridges; others blow them up. You take a man out of the gutter, but..."

"None of that!" Pierre cut him off. "We already agreed to forgive and forget."

"You guys don't get it, do you?" Watkins jumped up. "We had the world in the palm of our hands yesterday. We had the ambassador, the governor, the baron, all the movers and shakers, the soccer moms. Media coverage. These are the people who could get us what we want, set us up for life. Then he had to go lick the man down with a fastball."

Napoleon said, "Why do we have to kiss up to these people?"

"Those who have the power make the rules," Watkins answered sharply. "Our goal is to have a permanent place to play cricket. We have tried not to make race an issue, but race is like that proverbial white elephant in the corner. We have to be pragmatic…"

"Why you using all those big words on me?" Napoleon said.

"In simple language," Watkins said, "we are not only people of color in a white suburban world, but there are those who view us as outsiders. We have to play by their rules. If it means currying up to them, so be it."

"Watkins is being realistic," Pierre said to Napoleon. "And everything he has done has been with my blessing. He's lived and worked with these people. He knows how the system works. It's not a question of kissing up. He knows how to schmooze, how to romance the establishment to get what we want. He has my full confidence."

Pierre spoke with sincerity, but Watkins wasn't to be appeased. "It goes beyond yesterday's game," he said. "It's the whole league environment. It's gotten so nasty. And for what? As I told my neighbor Hankowsky last week, this is bush-league cricket. There aren't any selectors flying in from London or the Caribbean to take a look at how fast Napoleon bowls. There are no contracts to be signed. Nothing's at stake. So, why has it gotten this way?"

"I know where you're coming from," Pierre said. "You've worked hard for this club, giving up your nights and weekends, sneaking out on your wife. You and Pops kept this thing together all these years while other clubs came and went. Pops is out of the picture, and now you're the last link to the past."

"No one is indispensable," Watkins said.

"You are," Chong said.

"He's right," Pierre said. "I always tell the guys: I don't know how Watkins does it, or why he does it, because he hardly even gets to play. You leave the club, and there's no one to step forward to take your place."

"Look at Vijay Patel," Chong said. "We made him manager and his wife showed up at the grounds and embarrassed him in the worst way. Now, he can't set foot out of the house. He didn't even last a day as manager."

Pierre said, "You are it, my friend. Everywhere we go, people ask for you. Guys we haven't seen in donkey years, they ask for you. 'What about Watkins? Is he still with the club?'"

Chong said, "Last year, we went to that dance way, way up in Poughkeepsie. Met some of the old cricket guys. Gray as hell and still playing cricket. 'Where's Watkins?' they kept asking."

"Same thing in Buffalo, Staten Island and Connecticut," said Pierre. "You are it, my friend. A legend in your own time…"

"In his own mind," grumbled Napoleon.

"…Mr. Cricket in South Jersey, that's you," Pierre said. "I know your wife gives you hell, and I know you said you promised her you'd quit. But you love this game. For many, it's mere recreation. They can take it or leave it. For you, it's a disease you can't shake."

"Like an addict," Chong said. "Cricket is your fix."

"That's what it is," said Pierre. "Walk away and it would be like an addict trying to go cold turkey."

"Your wife tries to wake you up one morning and you're not moving," Chong said. "Stone cold dead. Another one gone."

They continued to work him over with their one-two punches, and deep inside Watkins knew they were right. He was a cricket addict, had been since, when he was four or five, his father made him a cricket bat from a coconut branch, and gently lobbed tennis balls to him. Gina was trying to make him go cold turkey and his club mates were dangling white powder in front of him.

Watkins felt the pull and tug, felt himself weakening. "I'll come back so we can proceed with our business plans, but on one condition." Watkins jabbed a finger at Napoleon. "He goes!"

"That's blackmail," Pierre said. "You don't blackmail the club."

"It's an ultimatum," Watkins said. "Him or me."

"And what if the majority says no?" Chong said. "This is a democracy, right?"

"Since when?" Watkins said. "All you want to know is when and where is the next game. I'm the one who made all the organizing decisions."

"Instead of treating the general here like a pariah, let's work with him," Pierre said. "Let's refine him. Don't embarrass the man, especially in front of people."

"I have feelings," Napoleon murmured. "You hurt my feelings up there on the Hill, man."

"You're an educated man," Pierre said to Watkins. "You made your living writing copy for advertisers, helping them communicate with their customers. Well, how about doing some *pro bono* work with one of your fellow West Indians? Napoleon here is a bit rough around the edges. Work with him…"

"All right, all right." Watkins thought they had made their case. He was a beaten man. "But if Napoleon wants to be a member of the club, he pays his dues like everybody else. We don't pay him."

"We've got to help him out until he gets straightened out," Chong said.

"What do you mean straightened out?" Watkins asked.

Chong said, "If you really want to know, the general jumped ship in Canada. A friend in Buffalo picked him up on the Canadian side of the border and brought him across. He missed the deadline to apply for amnesty by one day. Imagine that. One day. Pierre does a little immigration work on the side and is helping him get straight."

"That's a private matter," Pierre said. "If Napoleon wants to talk to Watkins about it, fine. Otherwise, let's move on."

Watkins gave up. They had him cold.

Napoleon asked whether he could leave, explaining that cancellation of the game between Fernwood and Pakistan meant he wouldn't be getting the $200 Pierre had promised him, a disclosure that caught Watkins by surprise. There was still time, Napoleon said, for him to find a team that could use his services.

"I invited Napoleon to this meeting because I wanted us to settle and put this thing behind us," Pierre said to Watkins. "How do you feel now about Napoleon?"

The way Pierre said it made Watkins feel guilty about the way he had berated his fellow West Indian. "Sorry if I hurt your feelings."

"That's okay, man," Napoleon said, with humility.

"I should have known better," Watkins said, rising to offer his hand.

This time Napoleon readily took it.

The two men embraced.

"That's more like it," Pierre said.

"You okay?" Watkins sought assurance from the big man.

"I'm okay," Napoleon assured him. "What about you?"

"I'm okay."

Chong said, "Now, let's talk about the future of the Fernwood Cricket Club."

Watkins took Napoleon's seat. "The club's dead in the water right now."

"I've already drawn up that injunction," Pierre said. "I'll file it in the morning."

"Not yet," Watkins said. "We went before council and got the shitty end of the stick. Now let's take our case to the man who controls the council, Mayor Quigley himself. We talk to him when he returns from his bereavement. In the meantime, how do you guys feel about building that gym?"

"You were supposed to talk to a financial planner and get back to us," Pierre recalled.

"I've gotten Siddique to draw up a business plan," Watkins reported. "I wasn't going to bother about it because of what happened yesterday. Now that you've pulled me back, I really think this is the way to go, long term."

He gave his best recollection of the plan.

Pierre and Chong were impressed with the bottom line.

Both men said they might be interested.

But they didn't think it would be easy getting their wives on board when it came to putting up their homes as collateral for the loan.

"I'll make copies of the business plan for everyone," Watkins said. "Show your wives the bottom line. What do you have to lose?"

They agreed they had nothing to lose and everything to gain.

"But I have to be honest with you; the only way this will work for me is if my wife is hired as the CEO, with an iron-clad contract," Watkins said.

"I know Gina; I don't have a problem," Pierre said, and turned to Chong. "Do you have a problem with that?"

"As a matter of fact, I do," the Black Chinaman replied. "His wife pretends, but I know she doesn't like any one of us. She thinks we're the ones wrecking your marriage."

"As I told Pierre, Gina isn't West Indian, so she can't relate to why grown men leave their wives on Sundays to play cricket throughout the summer," Watkins explained to Chong. "That could change if she got directly involved."

"And you haven't mentioned any of this to Gina yet?" Pierre asked.

"Not yet."

"How do you know she'll go for it?"

"Right now she's thinking of being a sales rep for Amway products," Watkins said. "That's small stuff. A gym catering to people like her would satisfy her own exercise routine and the business opportunity she's seeking. Her avocation becomes a vocation. The dream job."

"Man, you're really pumped up about this thing," Chong said.

"She'd love it," Watkins said.

"Not only that," Pierre put in, "but with her having a

financial stake in the company and running it, it gives you a chance to get back with the guys."

"That," Watkins said, "is one of the side benefits of the proposed Fernwood Cricket Company."

"Well?" Pierre challenged Chong. "How do you feel about our man Watkins back in the game?"

"We'll see how it goes," Chong replied, apparently not totally sold.

"I'll call the others and let them know what we decided," Pierre said. "My cousin is an architect. Maybe I can get him to design us the gym as a donation to the club."

"That would save us some money," Watkins said.

"So, when are you going to tell Gina about this?" Pierre asked.

"Saturday is my birthday," Watkins disclosed. "Gina normally takes me out for my birthday. I'll put the plan to her then."

"I'll do the same with Angie," Pierre said. "Why don't we set a deadline of noon Sunday to make a final decision based on our wives' reaction?"

And so it was decided.

******

"What's the matter with your hand?" Gina asked as Watkins walked in the door.

"I hit an immovable object. Nothing's broken. The doc at the hospital said it should be fine in a few days."

"Don't give me that nothing story. What happened?"

Watkins gave his spin on the incident, and had himself getting the better of Napoleon.

"You fought at a birthday party?" Gina shook her head in despair. "Oh, well, thank the Lord you've ended your affiliation with the club. What's that you're hiding behind your back?"

He showed her the dozen, fresh-cut roses.

She blushed. "What's the occasion?"

"Do I need an occasion to bring my wife roses?"

"Oh, Fred, you can be so sweet when you want to be." She kissed him on the mouth. As she looked around for a vase for the flowers, he whipped out a box of Godiva chocolates.

CHAPTER 8

Saturday May 12, a week later.

Watkins was awakened by a voice in his ear: "Happy birthday, young man."

Gina stood at the side of the bed, holding a breakfast tray with a covered dish and a newspaper.

"So, now I'm a young man," he said, rolling over and sitting up.

"Or would you prefer Mister Romantic?" she said, dreamy-eyed. "Flowers. Chocolate. Dancing at Bernie's. Special homemade dinners. And great sex." She actually blushed.

"That's the first time I've ever heard you use the S word."

"Losing my inhibitions at forty-eight?" She threw her head back with a laugh. "Better brush your teeth, before I start talking dirty to you."

"The minister's daughter?"

"Lately, I've learned a few choice words from Maggie. Go brush."

Gina set up the tray at the foot of the bed while be brushed, then watched him dig in.

"So," she said, replenishing his coffee, "where do you want to go for your birthday?"

"You decide," he said, sensing that she already had decided.

"Remember where we were when I said yes to your marriage proposal?"

"You don't forget something like that."

Gina unfolded the morning's edition of the Philadelphia Inquirer. She had circled a front-page headline:

Garden State Park's races will end soon.

The story was about the planned closing of the Garden State Park racetrack in Cherry Hill. It all came back to him as he read:

The advertising agency had won another creative award, and management decided to celebrate with an all-expenses-paid trip to the racetrack. He had invited her along. After losing twenty dollars on horses that never left the gate they slipped upstairs to the Phoenix Room. In the middle of their fine dining, she said she finally had an answer to his marriage proposal. She inhaled, held her breath, and closed her eyes.

They had been dating for three months. He had asked her to marry him on their first date and had professed his love for her at every opportunity since then. She seemed enthralled but unwilling to give voice to her feelings. He had ascribed her reserve, which bordered on formality at times, to her strict upbringing. It was clear she regarded marriage a serious matter and she wanted to be sure.

On this night, she would give her answer. She was about to break his heart. He was sure of it after she took that deep breath and in the silence that followed. He had thought of that possibility, was prepared to accept it, but thought it would be insensitive to tell him on a night of celebration for his creative efforts.

And when she started to tell him what a great guy he was, and how fortunate she was to have met him, bright, single and available, caring and romantic, he was convinced it was the preamble to the letdown.

"But?" he asked, in a choking voice.

She drew a deeper breath.

Was it that difficult to say no?

He tried to make it easy for her, and to cushion himself from the blow by expressing his appreciation for what they had shared. He was rambling so much while stirring the remnants of his gourmet meal that he wasn't sure he heard her answer correctly. Did she say, "I accept"? Or was it "I can't accept"?

He thought it was the former, but she had spoken so softly it was possible he hadn't caught the word "can't". Or could it be he hadn't wanted to hear it?

Her smile erased all doubt, a smile different from the others. She wanted to know if he still had the ring. He carried it each time they met, waiting for the moment.

In his exuberance and intoxication, he made the announcement of her acceptance to his ad-agency colleagues, and the word spread throughout the Phoenix Room, and total strangers began toasting their health and happiness.

Watkins nudged the flashback aside and looked up from the newspaper to his wife. The young woman he knew then was now a grandmother. She had aged well, much better than he had. Unlike him, she watched what she ate and her exercise routine had kept her fit. You had to look closely to see the streaks of gray in her hair.

Gina was smiling now as she was then. That soft, contented, radiant smile that captured the spirit of the woman. Their life as one had begun that night. It seemed only fitting that they return to a room filled with nostalgia. Another way to rekindle the spark before the bulldozers took down the racetrack to make way for a plaza.

******

Gina went to the hairdresser and returned with straightened hair tucked in at the back. Her head seemed to have shrunk and she was all face, fresh and shiny. She selected his favorite dress, a simple, black, strapless affair that hugged her without accentuating her lithe figure, that was cut low enough to reveal a necklace that caught the eye without being showy, and a glimpse of cleavage.

"What do you think?" She did a little pirouette before the full-length mirror.

"Special," Watkins said, admiring her all over again. "But it might be a bit chilly by the time we get back."

She agreed, and got a matching scarf.

They arrived at Garden State Park in time to check out the horses being saddled up in the paddocks and to watch them warm up for the first race. For the next two hours, Gina made bets on the friskiness of the animals, the color of the jockeys' silks, and birthdates of family members. Some of her picks turned into mules: They never left the gate. He, professing to know a thing or two about handicapping, bet on the basis of the history of the horses and jockeys, but fared no better.

"What was *that*?" Gina said after losing another two dollars, on Dancing Girl.

A hearse, followed by cars with "funeral" stickers in the windows, was coming down the dirt track.

"A regular, who wanted to be buried at the finish line," said a track loyalist next to her. "They're throwing his ashes onto the track."

"Yuck!" Gina said.

The ashes disappeared one race later, pounded into the dirt by nine horses, with Pinocchio out front. Gina picked the horse because she liked the name. She placed three two-dollar bets on Pinocchio, odds at 13-1.

Watkins watched his wife with deep satisfaction. Unlike their first visit more than two decades earlier, Gina had become highly animated. Her screams of "C'mon, c'mon," grew more intense as the horses came down the stretch with The Prince of Darkness, Run Around Sue, and the King of Spain closing in on Pinocchio. The horse on which he had bet, his namesake Freddie's Dream, was nowhere in sight.

In the end, it was Pinocchio by a nose.

"I won! I won!" Gina cried, jumping up and down in disbelief.

The payoff was $78, reducing their combined losses to $34.

Watkins cashed in their winnings and suggested they quit on the high note. "Otherwise, we'll be late for dinner."

Only then did they discover that the Phoenix Room had closed for good.

"What about the Lobster House?" Watkins suggested.

"Cape May?" Gina's eyes said yes, yes. Another memorable link to the past.

They held hands during the ninety-minute drive to Cape May. They got there at sundown. They gave their names, and asked for window seats. While waiting to be called, they strolled the docks where they had soft drinks and watched squawking seagulls follow the fishing boats coming in.

They got their old window seats overlooking the bay, where they could see the cruise vessels and sailboats come and go, the lights reflected in the water, and hear the waves lapping the wooden pilings beneath them.

Gina removed the scarf, baring her neck and arms and the swell of her bosom. She tossed her head back, girl like, though there was no hair in her eyes, and Watkins got goose bumps at her sensuality.

As they feasted on succulent lobster and crabmeat in linguine, crusty house bread and baked potato with sour cream, Watkins decided that the time had come.

He was about to unveil the business idea when a group of servers burst into song behind him. The servers came around to their table toting a lighted cake. The other diners in the crowded room joined in the "Happy Birthday" song as the cake was placed before him.

Watkins pretended to be surprised. He had seen his wife whisper to their server while he was studying the menu and suspected she had made the arrangements for the cake then. "What can I say? Thanks."

"You're so welcome." She bowed.

"Now, are you ready for *your* surprise?" he asked, with a hem and a haw.

"What surprise?"

"This may not be the right time...."

"Go ahead anyway."

Watkins took an extra deep breath. "I've done the research on the business idea I have for you. Something a bit more substantial than selling Avon and Amway products. It's something you and I can do together, something that would combine your interest in fitness with your desire to go into business. Here's what I came up with...."

He tried to be as casual about it as possible, between sips of strong, frothy Irish coffee. He hadn't brought the business plan, but there was no reason to: He knew the numbers by heart. He proceeded to write them down on napkins, the investments and projected incomes.

Gina stared at him, seemingly dumbfounded, while he wrote. Her silence continued long after he had finished.

"Well," he prompted, "what do you think?"

If looks could kill, he would have fallen over dead at that moment.

"Over the years you have taken my pots and pans, my salad bowls, my rakes and other garden tools down to your cricket field and never returned them," she said, in a low, sizzling voice that he had never heard before. "Now, you want to give away my house?"

Words, when he most needed them, failed him.

"Is that what you are telling me, Fred Watkins!"

"Hold on. I haven't told you the best part."

His initial presentation focused on the cricket club's needs, saving what he considered the best for last.

"Everyone is coming in as equal partners, but it would be all your show," he said, braving the daggers in her eyes and the heat of her heavy breathing. "You'd be the CEO. I'd take care of the marketing. Something we'd be doing together as you wanted, something that satisfies our personal and professional interests. But it essentially will be your show. The whole shebang."

"The whole shebang?"

"Everyone answerable to you."

"You scheming, conniving bastard!" Gina banged the metal lobster cracker on the table. The chattering around them stopped. "I was having a great time. I was thinking, finally I have gotten my husband back. But you haven't changed. You'll never change!"

She sprang up.

"Calm down, Gina," Watkins pleaded, unnerved by her reaction. "We're having a quiet conversation. There's no reason for this." The fire in her eyes told him that he wasn't getting through and that he was only compounding the problem by persisting. "Why don't I pick up the tab? We can take this up later."

Looking around for the waitress, he never saw the cake coming, but knew exactly what had hit him when it landed on his head.

When he cleared away the icing from his head and face and opened his eyes, Gina was gone. Diners who only moments ago had joined in the celebration of his birthday were snickering. Their waitress rushed up. She kept saying she was sorry, as though it were her fault, as she helped wipe icing off his head and sports jacket. Watkins demanded the bill and, unable to withstand the stares and snickers, marched off to the restroom.

Watkins fumed before the mirror as he completed the cleanup with paper napkins. He should have known better. To Gina, a home was more than a house. A home represented security, something you worked toward, and once you had it, it was to be handed down to your children and to their children. In her mind, Maggie one day would inherit it and she would leave it for their grandson, Edward.

He liked to think he was more business savvy, as savvy as the guys at the office. Back when the stock market was on fire, they borrowed money on the equity in their homes and invested it in the market. They made a killing buying and selling hot technology stocks. They paid off their loans and went on vacations and bought summer homes at the Jersey Shore and in the Poconos. Meanwhile, Gina hung on to her federally insured passbook accounts that paid her three percent interest, like those proverbial old ladies with memories of the Great Depression holding on to their AT&T and General Motors stock.

Talk about his making her angry! They could've been millionaires. Each time he brought up the subject, he got a patented answer: What if the stock market crashed? Yeah, and what if pigs could fly....

The waitress was waiting at the entrance to the restroom with the check. He gave her a hundred-dollar bill, told her to keep the change and went out in time to see Gina enter a Checker cab.

"Gina!"

The cab roared past.

Watkins had calmed down by the time he crossed the bridge and entered the Parkway. Maybe his approach was wrong. He had *told* her of the business plan and her role in it when he should have employed the art of suggestive selling by making her believe that the whole thing was her idea. Yes, he should have known better for an old advertising and PR man. He had screwed up big time. Then again, who knows, that approach also might have backfired.

Regardless, her public humiliation of him was inexcusable.

******

Watkins arrived at Gardenia Court as the Checker cab was coming out of the cul-de-sac. He saw Gina enter their front door, and the foyer lights go on. As he pulled into the driveway, the lights in the family room overlooking the driveway went on. He was walking toward the main entrance when he heard a loud cracking sound followed by a thump, and the sound of shattering glass. It came from the family room.

Watkins ran through the flower garden to the chin-high window and was aghast. Gina was swinging his prized cricket bat — the one given him for his "lifetime achievement" and autographed by club and league members — at the glass case with some of his cricket trophies and memorabilia.

"Gina!"

She turned her attention to the framed cricket images on the walls, taking aim at the autographed Hall of Fame poster of the West Indies national team players.

"Gina, no!"

The poster flew missile-like across the room on contact, and she went after it with upraised bat.

Watkins ran to the main entrance. The door yielded and he raced to the family room. The place looked as though a tornado had just touched down. There was no sign of Gina.

He heard a new thumbing sound below and skipped down to his basement office. The door was locked. The thumping, crashing sounds continued from inside.

He pounded the door. "Gina, open up!"

More shattering glass.

He found the right key on his key ring and opened the door. His bat was on the floor amid the ruins of more cricket memorabilia. No sign of Gina.

The rear door was open. He flicked on the high-intensity backyard lights, climbed the steps leading up to the yard, ran down the side of the house to the driveway, checked behind and under the two vehicles, examined the line of evergreen shrubbery against the front of the house. He observed that the front door was open and couldn't remember whether he had left it that way.

Watkins reentered the house through the front door and went from room to room, shouting her name with growing impatience, questioning her sanity. He rechecked the backyard and circled the property, returning inside to do a more thorough search, through closets, under beds and, standing on her new stepladder, the attic.

Convinced that she had fled the property, Watkins surveyed the neighborhood from the driveway. Front lights were on at all the houses. A light breeze fanned his face, but nothing stirred.

Watkins sat in the dark on the front steps, his anger building. He had devised a plan to save the club and at the same time satisfy her business interest. So she wasn't exactly thrilled about it. All she had to say was no, and that would have been the end of it. Why the Academy Award-worthy performance?

He felt the chill and went inside. The clock on the mantelpiece chimed twice: Watkins threw himself backward on the bed. Fear turned to guilt. What if something happened to her? Police statistics showed that the neighborhood was relatively safe. There were the occasional car theft and burglary and missing bicycles from front lawns, but no reports of personal attacks in the twenty-five years they had lived in Fernwood. But, he told himself, there was always a first.

Please, God, let her be safe.

He must have dozed off, for from somewhere far off came the sounds of soft chimes. Four of them.

Watkins again searched the house and grounds.

She had fled on foot, with no money, which meant she couldn't have gone far. He began calling the neighbors.

Roused from sleep, they wanted to know what time it was, claimed that they hadn't seen or heard from Gina, grilled him as to the nature of their fight, and made clear how they felt about the situation.

"You had it coming," said Mrs. Alvarez.

"What took her so long?" said Mrs. Meredith.

"Men!" sighed the divorced Mrs. Sandiford. "When will they grow up?"

Unable to sleep, Watkins got in the wagon. He cruised the neighborhood and drove down the boulevard. The neon lights for the Sunrise Motel burned just as brightly. Gina had no money, but her credit would be good at Bhattacharya's motel.

Bhattacharya's son was at the front desk watching a porno movie on a 13-inch TV on the counter. He hurriedly switched the TV off when Watkins walked in.

Surajit said that Gina wasn't there, and offered to check with "our affiliates" to see whether anyone matching her description had checked in.

No one had.

Watkins continued to make the rounds, stopping at neighborhood parks to scrutinize the bleachers and benches. The thought of Gina sitting, or even lying, ill-clad, on cold aluminum in sixty-degree weather was extreme, but no more so than her going ballistic in his den and fleeing with only the light clothes on her back.

He turned into Park Lane to Fernwood Park. Before him, clothed in darkness, was the source of all the friction between him and his wife. His cricketing days in America began here at this park, now being upgraded. It had been the source of immense joy, but here it must end.

He prayed: *Dear God, let her be safe. Return her to me, and I will start going to church regularly and be baptized, and be forever in Your service.*

Watkins sat straight up. Was it a mirage, or was that a human shape atop the bleachers near the broadcast booth?

He stumbled out of the wagon. Quivering with excitement, he drew near. He wasn't mistaken. Someone was seated up there. It had to be Gina. It was logical that she would be here. God had answered his prayers. Watkins stood trembling on the grass at the base of the bleachers and looked up at the figure less than ten feet away.

He filled his lungs. "I'm sorry. Please forgive me."

"Will you like to join me, Senor?" said a voice in a heavy Spanish accent.

Startled, Watkins stumbled back to his vehicle.

Continuing his search, Watkins became aware of the dark SUV about six car lengths behind. Several streets later it was still there. He waited at the next light, and the vehicle rolled to a stop alongside his wagon. Radio static emanated from within.

The youth behind the wheel said he was a member of the Neighborhood Watch on the graveyard shift. No, he hadn't seen anyone fitting Gina's description. "Do you wish to report her missing? I can call the cops for you."

Watkins thought about it. The police were unlikely to get involved unless foul play was suspected. And if foul play were suspected, her humiliation of him at the Lobster House would make him the prime suspect by providing the police with a motive. The fact that he was making inquiries about her whereabouts would be dismissed as an attempt to shift blame from himself.

"Thanks," he told the youth. "She's probably home by now."

She wasn't.

CHAPTER 9

Sunday, May 13

The phone rang, startling him. Watkins rolled over in bed and grabbed the receiver on the second ring.

"Can I talk to Mom?"

The sound of Maggie's voice deflated him. "Your mother's not here."

"Where is she?" Maggie demanded.

"I'll give her the message that you called, if she returns."

"What do you mean *if she returns*?"

He hung up. The phone rang as soon as he did. Watkins debated his options. He could come clean and tell Maggie that her mother had had it with him and fled, or he could stall in hopes that Gina showed up. Either way, there would be hell to pay with his feisty daughter. Might as well get it over with.

He answered, "Maggie, I've got some bad news for you…"

"What, your wife left you?" the caller answered and he recognized Michael Hankowsky's voice.

"How did you know?" Watkins asked his neighbor.

"It's all over the neighborhood," said the TV cameraman.

"Mary wouldn't happen to be harboring her, would she?"

"She isn't," Hankowsky said. "But my wife did want to come over and have a word with you. I talked her out of it."

"Why did she want to see me?"

"I took your advice and was nice to her, taking her bowling, then dinner. I presented her with the business plan then. She wanted to know whether I had lost it. And guess who ends up sleeping on the floor?"

"At least she didn't leave," Watkins said.

The calls kept coming in, and it didn't get any better.

"Cindy thinks you're going a little too far," the Englishman reported. "You already know we're up to our necks in debt." Asquith reported that he and Cindy had started the evening at Dickens Inn. He had loosened her up with a couple bottles of Boddingtons, then taken her fine dining at Le Bec Fin. He raised the subject over appetizers. They never got to the entrée, and she slept in the girls' room.

"At least she didn't kick you out of bed," Watkins said.

"No go," Pierre reported from his end. He had asked Angie on the dance floor at Bernie's, the popular supper club, as the tuxedoed pianist/singer crooned *Isn't It Romantic*. They never finished the Rogers and Hart tune, and she had left for her nursing job earlier than usual this morning to avoid speaking to him.

"Seems I've just wrecked a few marriages," Watkins sighed. "Including my own."

Pierre agreed that Gina's reaction was extreme. "She'll be back," he said, sounding a familiar note "They always come back.... Just so you'd know, I called Pakistan Cricket Club and told them to forget about rescheduling the game, that they can have the points. After what went down last night, I didn't think we could put together a team for today's game. They said they can accommodate us next Sunday."

Watkins wasn't interested, and told Pierre as much.

"We need to regroup," Pierre said.

"Not interested," Watkins said and hung up.

At 10 o'clock, he drove to the Fernwood Calvary Baptist Church. He parked well off the side of the road.

As he watched the members arrive for services, he more and more began to appreciate the things about Gina that he took for granted: waking to the smell of percolating Maxwell House master blend ("Coffee's ready; come and get it," she'd call out); nutritious, home-cooked meals replete with her fresh garden produce ("You have to have your veggies"); the dress clothes she bought for him from Today's Man ("Come try these on, Fred."); drawing his bath ("Is it warm enough?"); her fingers massaging sore muscles with baby oil ("How does *this* feel?"); the smell of her perfume, her softness beneath the sheet....

Watkins grew teary-eyed as he remembered.

He ended his scouting of the church around mid-afternoon, disheartened, after the men's choir members had locked up, and spent the rest of the day calling people listed in Gina's address book.

Hankowsky came over around 6 o'clock to "chill out" from Mary and to find out "how my man Watkins" was holding up. On learning that he hadn't eaten the whole day, Hankowsky went out and got Chinese and ate most of it while seated before the TV, watching the Philadelphia Phillies beat up on the New York Mets at home.

Watkins spent a restless night. Each time he fell asleep he thought he heard the front door open and close, or a car pull up into the driveway.

Had he really been that bad a husband?

Perhaps he should go see the shrink, have Sankar probe his mind to find out why, after all the promises, he risked his marriage by sneaking behind Gina's back, becoming a "scheming, conniving bastard," if he truly loved her. Could it be that his obsession for cricket was stronger than his love for Gina?

But to unload on the shrink would be to speak ill of Gina, and that was something he had never done. He had no doubt that Sankar respected the rule of confidentiality between doctor and patient and wouldn't breathe a word to the cricket community that the inscrutable Watkins was human, after all, but he couldn't risk it.

Watkins worked the phones most of the day, to no avail. Around 3 o'clock he made yet another round of the neighborhood, then drove to a diner to eat, not because he was hungry, but because he was starting to feel faint and thought he might collapse if he didn't eat.

Driving back home, Watkins tried to cheer himself up. He saw himself arriving home to find Gina in bed. She would be full of remorse, explaining that she had sought sanctuary at a neighbor's house and couldn't hold out anymore. She had time to think it over, and now realized what a nag she had been. Would he ever forgive her?

Watkins entered the house through the garage and heard muffled voices upstairs. Gina was back! She either was on the phone or had company. How should he handle this? Be a man and deflect the blame to himself? Or play the role of victim to the hilt? He decided to play it by ear.

The door of the master bedroom was ajar. The voices came from within. He listened and his heart sank: He had left the television on.

On entering, Watkins observed that the closet where Gina kept her formal clothes was open. He knew for sure he hadn't left it that way. The rack was bare. Everything else was in place, including her box of jewelry on the dresser top. He searched the box. A number of items, including the diamond choker he had given her for her last birthday, were missing.

He checked the house and saw no signs of forced entry.

Watkins' head spun as a new fear gripped him. Instead of cooling off, Gina had hardened. She had come home in his absence and taken her most expensive clothes and jewelry. Why those items? Had she concluded that now that she was a free woman, it was time to become the belle of the ball?

Maybe the next time he heard from her, it would be through her lawyer.

Was it *that* bad?

Why couldn't they sit down and talk it over?

To walk away like this meant that the good times they had shared didn't count. She couldn't possibly mean that. But she must have, because she was gone. He had thought her going ballistic in his den and rushing off into the night an impulsive action. Her returning to remove selective items was cold-blooded. Was she irrational? Or was that the sanest thing she had ever done since cricket came between them?

The phone rang. He recognized the number on Caller ID, but answered anyway.

"Lemme talk to Mom," Maggie demanded.

"There's something I have to say to you ."

"I'm not talking to you, Dad," Maggie interrupted. "Put Mom on the line."

"...and I'm coming to Manhattan to tell you in person what I have to say."

******

It was a ninety-minute drive north on the New Jersey Turnpike to midtown Manhattan, but Watkins opted to catch the Greyhound express from neighboring Mount Laurel. He thought the ride might relax him a bit, give him a chance to clear his head, to think through what he was about to say to his daughter. Maggie was as dominant as her mother was a pussycat, and this new development was likely to rupture forever their already contentious father-daughter relationship. But the closer the bus drew to the Big Apple the greater grew his anxiety over the inevitable showdown. By the time it pulled into the Port Authority, he was sweating.

The *sale* sign on the window of a toy store in the bus terminal caught his eye: *Buy one, second at half-price.* Watkins wandered in and emerged with two rubber ducks that quacked when squeezed. Two doors down, he bought and consumed a bottle of water, hoping it would cool down his nervous system. It didn't.

Emerging on the Eighth Avenue side, Watkins headed north in the gathering dusk, oblivious of the neon lights, the jostling crowds and the cacophony of sounds around him. Many moons ago, Manhattan, this avenue in particular, was home. Unlike many of his countrymen who settled in Brooklyn and Queens, he had arrived smack dab in the middle of Manhattan. It was a time of chaos - the Vietnam War, women's lib, flower children; smoking pot was cool, every other doorway along the avenue was a massage parlor, and prostitutes outnumbered pedestrians. Somehow he managed to stay focused with school and work. Then the Philadelphia job had beckoned, leading him to Gina.

Watkins walked more than a dozen blocks with leaden feet, retracing steps he had taken a thousand times, to 55th Street. From the pavement, he saw light in the fifth-floor apartment of the grimy building with the death traps for fire escapes.

The name Watkins was still on the mailbox for Apartment 5-A. He signaled his arrival by depressing the button next to the name three times in quick succession, then keeping it down for two more. Without waiting for the buzz, he plunged his old key into the lock of the massive iron door and turned.

The worn, ratty rug helped muffle the squeaks of each step of the stairs. Neither he, nor his uncle before him, had complained. It was understood that a ratty stairway was part of the price you paid for living in a rent-controlled building.

Watkins paused a few steps from the top to catch his breath. From overhead came the sound of a door being unlatched, and opened, then footsteps. A woman of twenty-something with shoulder-length braided hair, white sweater and dungarees appeared at the rails. She peered down past him.

"Where's Mom!" Maggie yelled.

Watkins boosted his energy level at will, and rushed up. Maggie moved to block him, but was a step too slow.

A short hallway, with cans of paint lined up against the walls, led to the living room. Furniture was piled up in the middle of the space and covered with plastic. The walls were bare.

Watkins looked around. "Who's the painter?"

"Never mind," Maggie said, locking the door behind them. "Where's my mother? Why isn't she here with you?"

A very dark man in a gray shirt and khaki slacks appeared in a doorway across the room and came toward him, all smiles. Watkins embraced his son-in-law, while complimenting him and Maggie for trying to transform the dump that he had maintained following his uncle's death and which he had sublet to them, at the same time cautioning that the improvements could be grounds for eviction. And once they were evicted, the landlord was sure to market the upgraded apartment as a luxury unit and quadruple the rent.

Kenneth assured him that they were doing it quietly so as not to arouse the neighbors' suspicion. They had continued sending the rent in Watkins' name to the same post office box number. The landlord had never come around to check the place in the two years they had been there.

Watkins opened the package and squeezed the ducks. "Two of the same," he said to Maggie. "Double the noise. Where's my grandson?"

Maggie snatched the plastic away. "Edward's asleep; please don't wake him."

"Expecting company?"

"Why?" Maggie said.

Watkins pointed to the dinner table in the adjoining room. "I see three sets of plates."

Maggie and Kenneth glanced at each other and Kenneth said, "Well, you did say you were coming."

"I didn't say what time."

"That's not for you." Maggie brushed past him and turned one of the plates over. "Why aren't you answering the question, Dad? Since Saturday I've been calling and can't get an answer. That's not like Mom."

Watkins glanced uneasily at Kenneth.

"I'll finish up in the kitchen," Kenneth said.

Watkins went the other way, to the balcony overlooking the avenue. Maggie followed, accusing him of acting strangely and demanding to know what was going on.

Watkins held the rail to steady himself. "Your mother has left me." He stood with his back to her, braced for the onslaught. Instead, he heard laughter.

"Oh, please, Dad, be real," Maggie said. "Mom will never leave you. I don't know why, but she'll never leave you."

"She did. We went to the Lobster House in Cape May for my birthday. We had a fight. She took a taxi home, went postal in the family room and my office and fled."

"What did you fight about? And don't tell me it was over that silly game of yours."

"Cricket is not a silly game." Regardless of what he had said to his wife to trigger her extreme reaction, regardless of the consequences of what he had done, don't make light of the game. Attack him, yes, but not the game.

"You're a lousy father and husband," Maggie said. "Gone every weekend, April through September. Everything stops for cricket. I'm surprised you even had a marriage."

He wasn't going to deny it. "She's mad at me, but what I don't understand is why she hasn't gotten in touch with you, at least to let you know she's safe."

"She must still be mad at me. It's just like her. She criticizes you but whenever I join in the criticism, she dumps on me."

"Maggie, what are you talking about?"

"You and Mom were supposed to be here last weekend, remember?" she said. "Mom and I were going to do things together. You and Kenneth were supposed to take Edward out. But you decided that that game on the Hill before so-called royalty was more important. I blamed her for letting you get away with it. A bunch of grown men in white uniforms running back and forth, back and forth, up and down, for seemingly no reason."

As she spoke, Maggie moved like a caged animal from one end of the balcony to the other in an impromptu skit of how batsmen score runs. She stopped, "Howzat, Umpire!" she said to a make-believe umpire, and stuck a finger up. "Out! Leg Before Wicket!" She grimaced, the reaction of irate batsmen when given out LBW. "Oh, God, no! No! I ain't out!" she said in a put-on Jamaican accent. She assumed a stiff upper lip. "I'm the bloody umpire, and it's not cricket to question the umpire's decision," she said in a nasal, British accent.

The skit grew wilder. She accurately captured the antics, replete with authentic accents, of her imaginary Pakistani, Indian, British and West Indian batsmen and bowlers. Maggie had done it once before, during happier times, and he thought it hilarious. Now he felt she was trivializing the game, and mocking, rather than entertaining, him.

"At least you remember," Watkins said, with a sigh. "We used to do things together as a family. From the very beginning of our relationship, she came out to the games." He could see Gina, early spring, on the steps of the club-house at Haverford College that picture-perfect Saturday. Her first look at the game. Hair styled in a mini Afro, Cardigan sweater and jeans, standing to cheer lustily each time he whacked one over the trees and into the duck pond. He was in his prime then, in top form, and the weak opposition bowling gave him a chance to show off his strength like a proud peacock. "You probably were too young to remember, but your mother was once a club mate. She did the books, and played in some games. When you were born, we brought you out, as well."

"I remember, all right," Maggie said. "I remember you dragging us around New Jersey and Pennsylvania and across Staten Island, stopping to use dirty bathrooms at gas stations, forcing us to sit on hard, metal bleachers in the hot sun. And the people on the bleachers are talking in this fast Jamaican language and carrying on. And the part mommy couldn't take: They were talking about you when you were on the field. Do you want to know what one of your best friends said about you?"

"No, I don't." He really didn't care. Behind-the-back criticism was part of the game. You expect it.

"He said you were losing your eyesight, that's why there were all those zeroes next to your name in the score-book."

She was baiting him, seeking to drive a wedge between him and his club mates. He wasn't going to fall for it. He was here to discuss her mother, and enlist her support in finding Gina. Nothing more.

"He said that you had become the weakest link on the team," Maggie said.

She had to be making that stuff up. No way was he ever the weakest link. He would lose his form from time to time, but that was to be expected.

"Still don't want to know which one of your so-called friends said that of you?" Maggie seemed to have sensed his sudden discomfort. She had stuck the knife in his back and was eager to twist it.

"No, I don't." It was all part of the territory. You give as much ribbing as you get.

"It was Chong!" she said. "Fitzroy Chong."

"The Black Chinaman said that of *me*?" Watkins felt a stab of pain as she twisted. He would deal with Chong later. "I know what you're trying to do."

"It's true, isn't it?" Maggie continued to rant. "Mom tells me it has gotten a lot worse since then. You hardly even get to play anymore. You do all the work and yet you don't get picked on the team. The only reason you haven't quit is because you want to feel important."

"Your mother said that?" It would be out of character for Gina to say something like that, he thought. He and Gina had been careful in presenting a united front against Maggie. They defended each other whenever she tried her Mom-against-Dad, conquer-and-divide attempt to have her own way. "Or is that what you *think* she believes?"

"I know how your mind works!" Maggie said. "You say to yourself, 'I am important because I can get all these things done.' And your cricket buddies say, 'You know what, let him come to the game, and bring the gear and roll out the carpet, and push that heavy roller up and down the wicket, and put up the flags, because we need somebody to do this crappy job. Nobody has time to do it, and nobody is willing to do it, so let Watkins do it.'"

Watkins conceded to himself that her words had a ring of truism, but he couldn't afford to let her beat him down. "Maggie, I know I have a problem. I don't need your amateur psychoanalysis."

"Then go see a real shrink," she snapped. "He'd tell you the same thing. I'm saving you money."

Watkins felt a new bout of depression coming on. He staggered to the far end of the balcony, looked down and saw a big, red blur. What if he jumped? He could almost hear Mrs. Alvarez and his other Fernwood neighbors venting to reporters that they always thought he was a bit strange, and that they could never figure out what a nice lady like Gina saw in him.

"Your mother has never understood."

"Oh, you poor, poor thing." Maggie had stepped down from her soapbox and was pooh-poohing, with pouted lips. "'My wife doesn't understand me,'" she added in singsong.

"Maggie, if you aren't going to take me seriously, there's no point to this conversation."

"Okay, Dad." Maggie folded her arms and leaned back. "Tell me: what's to understand?"

"People born in this country have many options when it comes to sports."

"Uh-hum," she droned.

"Don't mock me!"

"I'm listening."

"They have baseball, soccer, hockey, basketball, football, and those are just some of the professional sports. What do we have?" He hadn't come here seeking sympathy, wasn't trying to get her on his side. This was all about solution of a problem he had identified, and if Maggie could be objective for a second, then she could help bring about that solution.

"Cricket," he said. "That's all we have. West Indian women understand that. They, too, grew up with the sport. Take Pierre. His wife is Antiguan. She may not like the idea of her husband being away from home every weekend, but she doesn't denigrate the sport or her husband because of his love for the game."

"What are you saying?" Maggie leaned precipitously over the rail and craned her neck, trying to look him in the face. "That you wished you had married a West Indian woman?"

"I'm just telling it the way it is," he said. "The fact is West Indian immigrants in the suburbs who grew up on cricket are very isolated. If we lived in the inner cities it might be different. We'd be running constantly into our people in the barbershops, the grocery store, the hole-in-the-wall restaurants, the churches. There'd be carnivals, dances, domino tournaments, and lots of other cultural diversions."

"You moved to the suburbs because you wanted to be part of the American dream," she said. "Nice homes, better schools, less crime. That's what you told me."

"But there's a downside to the suburbs for people like me," he said. "I cut the grass one day a week, then what?"

"You can start going to church, like Mom wants you to," she said.

"Church is only a couple hours on Sundays," he pointed out. "There has to be more to life than cutting the grass on Saturdays and going to church on Sundays."

"And cricket is life?"

"Cricket," he said. "is what defines us. It's who we are. It is the reason we seek out one another on weekends. You're half West Indian. Surely you understand that."

"I'm half nothing." Maggie drew back as though the comment were an affront to her sensibilities. "I'm American. African American. One hundred percent born and bred. My roots are here, like my mother's. You've been in this country for more than thirty years. That's time enough to have lost whatever longing you have for the past."

"Some things, Maggie, are innate in you," Watkins said. "Remember the movie *Citizen Kane*? Here was this character, played by Orson Welles, a man of wealth and influence. What's the last word that comes out of his mouth before he dies? *Rosebud*. His entire life summed up in one word. *Rosebud*. And who, or what, was Rosebud? A little sled with which he used to play in the snow as a kid."

"And cricket is your Rosebud?"

"You can call it that."

"Ha!" Maggie cried. "I can see it now: you, lying on your deathbed, your wife by your side, and just before you slip away, you look her in the eye. She waits for you to call her name, to say you love her, and what comes out? 'Cricket!'"

"Now you're just like your mother," Watkins groaned. "You don't even try to understand."

"No, you, Dad, are the one who doesn't understand." Maggie spun him to face her and shoved him against the sliding glass door. It vibrated. "Mom was the one who took me to the church picnics, to the pool, to Girl Scout meetings, to the parades. She was the one who removed the training wheels from my bicycle and helped me up each time I fell off my two-wheeler. She was the one who held me up in the pool while I splashed about. Even though you weren't there when I was little, it wasn't so bad for her. At least she had someone to talk to, to do things with, even if it was just hanging around the pool to talk to the other moms.

"When I left for college, and then got married and left home, it was like I didn't need her anymore. Mom didn't say it, but I could tell in so many ways that that was how she felt. Something inside her died a little as I guess happens when daughters leave home. With me gone, Mom looked more and more to you to fill that void. But you always worked late and when you came home you either were too tired or you wanted your quiet space to write that never-ending whodunit of yours. And summer weekends, forget it.

"So now Mom's waiting for you to retire so you can spend some quality time together. Finally, you have retired but it's just as bad. While you're off rose-budding with your cricket buddies, Mom's looking at her life and she's saying 'You know what, I'm forty-eight years old, my daughter is gone and my husband doesn't need me anymore because all he does is hang out with these crazy Jamaicans and Asians whom I don't understand anyway — the way they carry on — so what's the point? I might as well pack up and leave.' Don't you see it, Dad?"

Watkins felt the guilt creeping back in, and shifted his gaze to the giant blur in the avenue below. Maggie had just made him see things through a different lens. Life had always been on his terms, and Gina went along for the ride, her feelings and desires secondary. But he refused to believe he had been that bad a husband.

"You talk as though her entire universe revolves around me," he said. "She does have her circle of friends."

"That's fine," Maggie said. "And Mom doesn't mind your having a night out with the boys every once in a while. Not every weekend, spring through fall. Weekends are when you go places together."

"We did go to the Lobster House on Saturday. I even came up with a business idea for her. It was something we could do together. That's what set her off."

"Ha!" Maggie scoffed. "Mom told me about your going to the Lobster House, but then you had to ruin the evening with your harebrained scheme to put the house up as collateral for a loan for your cricket club. You told her she'd be managing the whole shebang. The only shebang she's controlling is her own household. Kenneth and I will be inheriting that house one day, and we expect it to be free and clear. So, you can junk that idea."

Maggie continued to rant, but he wasn't really listening because it was more of the same, attacking him, instead of the problem, but her words must have been registering somewhere in his subconscious.

"What did you say?" He confronted her, his entire body throbbing.

"I said it's time you wake up and smell the roses with your wife."

"No, the part about the Lobster House and my harebrained scheme…"

Her eyes avoided his, just for a moment, while she

tried to think her way out of it. "Mom called Saturday morning and said she planned to take you to the Lobster House for your birthday."

"Oh, Maggie, Maggie, Maggie," he said. "Why are you putting me through the wringer like this?"

"I don't know what you're talking about," she said, but the feistiness was gone.

"Maggie, your mother couldn't have told you on Saturday morning about dinner at the Lobster House because we didn't decide to go to Cape May until after — after, my dear — we had gotten to Garden State Park and discovered the Phoenix Room restaurant was closed. That means she would have spoken to you *after* she went ballistic in the house and fled."

The game was up, and Watkins was both angry and relieved. The major pieces of the puzzle were in place; the rest was easy to figure out. "She called you from one of the neighbor's houses, didn't she?" He wondered which one. The Hankowskys were next door and Mrs. Alvarez across the cul-de-sac. Theirs were the closest homes. He deducted that it was his Hispanic neighbor, for the TV cameraman would have squealed on his wife. "You picked her up early yesterday. This morning, when I was out, you came to the house and picked up her things."

Maggie stared in stony silence. Her slip of the tongue had made her immobile.

"What's the matter?" Watkins said, with satisfaction. "Cat got your tongue?" He looked past her to the kitchen table. "I take it that that third plate on the table is hers. Where are you hiding her? In Edward's room? Let's find out."

"Okay, you win." She sighed. "You win."

You win, she had said. It was a rare concession, and he would have treasured it at any other time. But this was no game to him. Then he blamed himself for not having read the clue early: At no time had Maggie expressed concern for her mother's welfare.

"I did pick her up from one of the neighbors', but I'm not going to tell you who." The combativeness had returned. "And I did come back and pick up some of her things. I was going to dress her up, and take her out to meet men! Lots of men! Handsome, available men who would show her the appreciation you never did."

"Now, *you* be real," he said. "All handsome, available black men have been taken."

"Who said anything about their being black?"

"You, Mrs. Black Pride, introducing your mother to a non-brother?" Watkins laughed at the contradiction. "You, a woman's rights activist thinking that the solution to a woman's problem is finding other men! That's a riot." He laughed even louder. "May I go rescue my wife from whatever evil spell you have cast over her?"

"You wait here." Maggie retreated backward from the balcony, and closed and locked the sliding door when he tried to follow.

Kenneth unlocked the prison and came in. "Little rough on you, huh?" he said, with that cool smile. I thought you could use this." Kenneth held out a glass. "Your special: rum and Coke."

He didn't realize how thirsty he was until he put the glass to his lips.

"For what it's worth," Kenneth said, "Gina's very remorseful. Didn't think what she did was very Christian. Wanted to go back home the moment she arrived. Maggie wouldn't let her."

"Thanks." As immigrants with a good work ethic, married to American women, and with a strong sense of family, he and Kenneth related well to each other. It hadn't always been that way. He had had his doubts about Kwankwo Kanu when Maggie, much to their consternation, married the Nigerian in her sophomore year at Rutgers the day he graduated with a degree in business accounting. Kanu's student visa had expired. He and Gina had had their doubts not only as to the Nigerian's motive in marrying Maggie, they also were unsure whether their Afro-centric daughter married for love, as she professed, or because she loved the idea of marrying a brother from Africa. Two years later, they had concluded that Kwankwo, renamed Kenneth by students who kept butchering his first name, and Maggie were a perfect fit. Kenneth was as unflappable as Maggie was volatile.

Watkins knew that his son-in-law was trying to be nice with the offer of a drink and comments about Gina's remorse, maybe even score points with the old man. Or, knowing that Maggie was firmly in her mother's corner, Kenneth wanted to even things up a bit. We men are supposed to stick together, aren't we? But Watkins felt this was something he and Gina needed to work out themselves if Maggie would let them.

As usual, Gina's perfume preceded her.

Watkins pretended not to be shocked by what he saw. Gina had let her hair down. Her lips were painted a deep red, matching the color of her shoulder-less, skin-tight sequined dress that barely covered her bosom and reached to the floor.

"Hi," she said, barely above a whisper.

Maggie stood behind her mother like a designer presenting a model with her latest creation, and Watkins knew that this new Gina had to have been his daughter's creation, her idea of proof that Mom had intended to paint the town red.

"Do you know how much heartache you've caused me?" Watkins asked his wife.

"Oh, Dad!" Maggie stepped to her mother's side. "You had your chance and you just blew it!"

"What did I do?" Watkins asked, exasperated.

"You are the perpetrator, and you're acting as though you're the victim," Maggie accused.

Kenneth excused himself.

"Maggie, can I talk with my wife?" Watkins said. "Alone?"

"No, you can't!"

"It's okay, Maggie," Gina said to her. "I'll be all right."

"No, you won' be. He's as slippery as an eel. I'm here to make sure you don't give him any wiggle room."

"Girl, I can handle myself."

"No, you can't!" Maggie pushed her mother backward into the living room and Watkins again became a locked-down prisoner.

The door was hardly soundproof. Watkins heard the heated debate on the other side of the glass. Gina was, indeed, remorseful, and wanted to redeem herself by giving him one last chance. Maggie accused her mother of being softhearted and called him undeserving. Gina said that was a little too strong. Maggie wanted to know what had he ever done for any of them. He was a good provider, Gina said. Maggie went "Ha!" and said he was never home. Gina answered that he was the one who made it possible for her to sign up for swimming lessons, and ice-skating, and jazz dance, and piano lessons, and acting and art classes, and kung fu, and learning to play the flute and the tuba, an instrument she could hardly lift and never learned to play; that she had to have it all, though her interest lasted no longer than a Joe Louis fight. Maggie told her mother to wake up, that she never asked to be born, but that once she was born it was her father's responsibility to provide for her. Gina said at least give him the credit for that, that even now he showed he cared by allowing her to have the apartment. Maggie said she was the one paying the rent, and Gina answered yes, but he gave up the profit he had been making subleasing it to others to let her have it. At this point, Maggie broke down and cried and asked why Gina always took his side, and said that next time she would know better than to rescue her.

The two women in his life hugged, kissed, made up and returned to him, Maggie carrying the two plastic ducks he had bought for Edward.

"These," Maggie said, holding up the gift, "are two toys." She squeezed them. They quacked. "I had lots of toys like these. That was when I was a child. I spoke as a child then; I understood as a child; I thought as a child: But when I became a woman, I put away childish things." She handed her mother the toys.

Her words had a familiar ring to them. "Shakespeare?"

"No, Dad," Maggie said, chastising. "You wouldn't know where that came from because you don't know the Bible. It's from the New Testament, 1 Corinthians, Chapter 13, Verse 11."

"I was close."

"I'm not joking with you, Dad!"

"Sorry," he said, rolling his eyes in Gina's direction.

"Your problem, Dad, is that you never grew up," Maggie said. "You're fifty-five years old and you are hanging around kids young enough to be your grandchildren. It's time to put away your toys. Because if you don't you won't be getting a second chance. I'm telling you here and now that the days of my mother playing the long-suffering wife are over. Either you straighten up and fly right or you're history!"

Watkins raised his right hand, showing them his open palm. "It will be different, I swear to God."

"Not to God," Maggie said. "God is a merciful God. I'm not."

"I swear to you."

"That's better," Maggie said. "Now, let's have dinner."

Maggie marched off. Gina started to follow. Watkins reached out and drew her into his arms. The ducks got caught between them and quacked. They laughed. She put the plastic down and they embraced. He felt her warmth and her rapid heartbeat. She hugged him back. He kissed her lips and told her he was sorry. She said she, too, was sorry, that she didn't know what got into her, smashing the memorabilia and pictures he had collected over the years.

He silenced her with a finger across her lips. "Those things are replaceable; you're not."

"Stop fornicating back there!" Maggie called out from the dinner table. "The food's getting cold."

Gina let go. "Can't wait to sleep in my own bed. Maggie can be overbearing. The last straw was forcing me to wear this dress."

"To paint the town red with young available men?"

"She also has a wild imagination." Gina giggled. "Wonder who she got it from. Better change before I suffocate."

Gina went into Edward's room and emerged in the black, sleeveless Saturday night dress and necklace. He thought she was making a statement. She was rolling the clock back. This time, they were going to get it right.

"Dad will say grace," Maggie commanded. "And keep it short, I'm hungry."

Watkins thanked the Lord for reuniting them as a family, then sought His blessing on the baked chicken and potatoes, corn bread, gravy, with tossed salad, and a special blessing to the preparers of the food.

"That was very nice, Dad," Maggie said. "Kenneth, will you pass me the corn bread?"

Watkins stole shy glances at his wife across the table, and caught her doing likewise on the sly, and when their eyes did meet she smiled that demure, schoolgirl smile of hers, and he thought she never looked more beautiful.

In the bedroom, Edward was crying.

Watkins rose and went and got him.

When he emerged with the toddler in his arms, there was a cake in the middle of the table with a lighted candle, and his family members were saying "Happy birthday to you."

Watkins guessed it was Gina's idea when she learned he was coming. Yes, this time they'd get it right.

Maggie relieved him of the baby to allow him to blow out the candles and cut the cake while Kenneth took pictures.

"Another thing, Dad," Maggie said. "I know you think church is for old people. If that's so, you now qualify."

"That reminds me," Kenneth said. He left the room and returned with a fat envelope. "Happy birthday, Dad."

Watkins hefted it. Money?

It was his membership card for the American Association of Retired Persons, along with literature detailing his membership benefits and coupons for discounted airline tickets and a host of goodies.

Maggie said, "A good place to start is with one of those once-in-a-lifetime cruises that normal people — hear that, Dad, normal people — take when they retire. You eat all these sumptuous meals and dance in the middle of the ocean under the stars."

"I'd like that," Watkins said, deeply appreciative of the gift. "But ever since your mother saw the movie *Titanic* she has been afraid to go on water because she can't swim."

Maggie accused him of making it up. Gina confirmed it was true, and Maggie said, "There you go again, taking his side," and while the two women in his life butted heads Watkins helped Kenneth clear the tables, then went to wash up.

Watkins smiled at the man who looked back at him in the bathroom mirror. He certainly felt like a new man. Gina was back in his arms. What more could he ask?

His cell phone rang.

Caller ID said it was Pierre.

"Did Gina come back?" Pierre inquired.

"Everything's fine," Watkins assured the club president. "Thanks for asking."

"I told you she'd be back," Pierre said. "Now you can refocus on getting the cricket club back on track."

"You caught me at a bad time; let's talk later." Watkins flipped the cell shut, pocketed it and rejoined his family.

The Fernwood Cricket Club, an organization he had founded a quarter-century ago and that had been such an integral part of his life, was back at square one, without a place to play at home. But that wasn't his concern.

At least, not at *this* very moment.

He needed first to savor his reconciliation with Gina before even *thinking* of embarking on another clandestine misadventure to save his cricket club from going down the tubes.

COMING SOON:

EWART ROUSE

STICKY WICKET
Vol. 3

watkins' final inning

Printed in the United States
202068BV00002B/103-183/P